THE SECRET OF MARIE

REBECCA BRICKER

The Secret of Marie

ISBN: 1518839320
ISBN-13: 9781518839320
Library of Congress Control Number: 2015918374
CreateSpace Independent Publishing Platform
North Charleston, South Carolina

Cover graphic design by Elizabeth MacFarland

Front cover:
Theodore Robinson, *La Débâcle*, 1892,
The Ruth Chandler Williamson Gallery,
Scripps College, Claremont, California

Back cover:
Theodore Robinson, *The Layette*, 1892,
The Corcoran Gallery of Art,
Washington, D.C.

Theodore Robinson, *Self-Portrait*, c. 1884-87,
The Metropolitan Museum of Art,
New York

Theodore Robinson, *A Marauder,* 1891,
The San Diego Museum of Art,
San Diego, California

Photographs by Theodore Robinson used with permission
by the Terra Foundation for American Art, Chicago

To the village of Giverny

ALSO BY REBECCA BRICKER

Tales from Tavanti:
An American Woman's Mid-Life Adventure in Italy

Not a True Story

AUTHOR'S NOTE TO READERS:

Promise yourself you won't read the epilogue before you finish the book. It contains the final twist of this little mystery.

Image of Marie:
Theodore Robinson, *The Layette* (detail, p. 216), c. 1892

1

Giverny, France
2004

There were no other guests at the moulin that night. It was late September, the end of the tourist season in Giverny. Gérard, the proprietor, lived elsewhere in the village.

I had the entire inn to myself that night – or so I thought.

Two of the participants in the painting course, who were staying at the lodge on the hill above the village, walked with me down the moonlit lane to the moulin, an old mill made of timber and stone.

The night air was cool and crisp, tinged with a smoky autumn scent. A nearly full moon hung in the bare branches of the cluster of poplar trees that stood on the banks of the little stream that turned the moulin's water wheel.

Tom held a flashlight, as I fumbled with the padlock on the moulin's front gate. "Do you want us to come in with you?" he asked.

"No, that's okay. I'm going straight to bed."

"Will you be joining us for breakfast?" Alyce asked.

"I'll come up after. Gérard said he'd bring pastries in the morning."

"Call if you need anything," Tom said. "You have my number, right?"

"I do." I patted his arm. "I'll be fine."

"See you in the morning." Alyce gave me a hug.

Bonne nuit and *sleep well* floated in the air as Alyce and Tom disappeared into the darkness.

The gate creaked on its rusty hinges. I latched the padlock and gave it a hard tug to be sure it was secure. I was in for the night – almost.

My heart jumped as the security light went out. I waved my arms, hoping to trigger the motion sensor. Success. I laughed at my bird-like shadow on the stone wall – wings flapping wildly. I could see perfectly well without the floodlight. The moon was bright. Lights inside the moulin were welcoming me. But I felt reassured to have a light at my back as I walked across the courtyard.

A *chouette* cried out, as if to say, *You are not alone.* She sounded more like a loon than her owl cousins who lived in a deodar cedar tree in the backyard of the house where I had lived in southern California.

I unlocked the front door and slipped inside the entryway, then quickly set the bolts.

I was staying in the moulin's grand guestroom upstairs. The room had a 15-foot vaulted ceiling, an immense arched window and a wrought-iron canopied bed that belonged in a fairy tale.

But I didn't head straight to my room. I thought I should look around. Just to be sure I was really alone.

I climbed the stairs of the moulin's tower, turning on lights and peeking behind doors. I lingered in each of the guest rooms, admiring the talents of Gérard's decorator. French quilts called *boutis* draped the antique beds.

There was one last door on the top floor, which I thought would open into a bathroom. Instead, I found myself at the foot of a dark stairwell leading to the attic. A rush of cold air embraced me. It wasn't really a draft or a breeze from an open window. It was more like a *presence*. I slammed the door tight and hurried downstairs.

There had been a phantom of the opera, after all. Perhaps there was a phantom of the moulin.

I sat on the edge of my fairy-tale bed, looking at a sealed trap door, high on the wall above me. I wondered what was behind it and why it was there.

I could hear water splashing over the paddle wheel just below my room. I shivered.

Enough, I told myself. I always had been a great teller of ghost stories in my youth. But I didn't especially like starring in one myself.

I stood in the center of the room, closed my eyes and sang George Gershwin's *Summertime*. I sang it as the soothing lullaby it's meant to be. Directly under the peak of the vaulted ceiling, I felt an exhilarating resonance as I sang.

3

I walked around the room, still singing, and opened the window in the bathroom. The *chouette* sang, too, from her perch somewhere in the treetops.

That night, I slept like a princess in my fairy-tale bed.

~

When I opened the curtains of the arched window the next morning, the courtyard was shrouded in fog that had rolled in from the Seine. The radiator under the window was stone cold. I grabbed a sweater and headed downstairs.

Gérard had set a place for me at the long wooden table in the dining room. Since I was the only guest, I had asked him for a simple breakfast – no fuss. There was a bowl of fruit on the table, along with a plate of cheeses, homemade jam and a basket of croissants. The perfect French breakfast – *le petit déjeuner*, the little lunch.

As I sat down, Gérard appeared in the doorway to the kitchen carrying a tray with two steaming mugs and a small pitcher of frothed milk.

He was in work clothes. His faded denim shirt was splattered with yellow paint. "Did I wake you?" he said. "I'm sure you heard the ladder fall."

"I hope you weren't on it."

"No, but such a mess…"

His young chocolate Labrador sheepishly appeared in the doorway. Her fur looked damp from a bath.

"Reste! Stay." Gérard shook his head. "She was a yellow dog a few minutes ago." He handed me a mug. "Milk?"

"*Merci.*" I took the pitcher and poured, spooning a dollop of froth onto the dark French roast.

He sat down with a sigh. "So how did you sleep, all alone in the moulin?"

"I checked under all the beds, I must admit."

Gérard laughed. "So I don't need to give you a tour."

Lines creased his ruggedly handsome face. It looked like he had combed his thick brown hair with his fingers that morning. He had big, strong hands – tinged with yellow paint at that moment – but there was a gracefulness and gentleness about them. I tried to picture Gérard in his old life, as an architect in London. My friend Nicole, who ran the art school at the lodge, had told me a little bit about him. He came from an affluent Giverny family, attended university in Paris and had worked in London for many years at an international architectural firm – explaining why he spoke perfect English with a British accent. He had been engaged to an English woman, but suddenly broke it off last year, a few months before the wedding, and came back to Giverny. He bought the moulin and threw himself into renovating it as a B&B.

I looked up at the massive ceiling beams, richly stained and varnished. Nicole said the place had been a mess when Gérard bought it. "You've done an amazing job."

"Some call it Gérard's Folly. Maybe that's what I should have named this place."

"Who's your decorator?"

"A woman in Paris. A friend."

"She has great taste. I love the furnishings. Especially that bed I'm sleeping in."

"We found it at a market in Brittany. Some of the antiques are from my family."

"And the *boutis*?"

He looked surprised. "You know about *boutis*?"

"I love quilts. I have a *boutis* on my bed at my apartment in Paris. A quilt changes the feel of a room."

Gérard smiled. "That's what Julie says."

He handed me the croissant basket. "Henri, our village baker, has been making these for 40 years. Since I was a kid."

I could feel butter melting on my fingertips as I broke one in half.

"And the jam?" I asked, helping myself to a generous spoonful.

"My mother's. From her pear trees."

I sank my teeth into the croissant and was suddenly dusted with pastry flakes.

Gérard took one from the basket. "I have no willpower. I've already had two this morning." He slathered his with jam. "God, Henri, you're killing me." He took a big bite.

"Heaven," I said.

Gérard nodded. We savored the buttery bliss.

I looked out the dining room windows to a pasture beyond the stream. The fog was burning off. Dew glistened on the grass in the pale vapory light. "This truly is heaven." I smiled at Gérard. "Thanks for letting me stay. I know it's the end of the season for you."

"I'll close up for the winter in a few weeks. But it's nice to have some company, if you don't mind a little background noise."

Gérard looked at his dog, who lay in the doorway with her head on her paws. "*Oui*, Coco?"

She jumped to her feet, wagging her tail, clearly wanting to come to him.

"*Viens, chérie.* Come," he said softly. She bounded toward him and nuzzled his cheek as he bent down. Fondly, he said to her, "We must kiss and make up."

~

Patches of fall color looked like bold painted brushstrokes on the hillside, as I walked up the road to the lodge.

It was my first visit to Giverny, but it felt familiar to me. I had studied European art history in college and fallen in love with French Impressionism. A poster of Claude Monet's water lilies hung in my dorm room back then. But I hadn't imagined that one day I would stand by the pond where he had painted that scene.

I couldn't have imagined it even six months ago. For 10 years I'd been in L.A., working as a freelance writer. I had a comfortable life, lots of friends. But I was restless and turning 40 – a dangerously exciting combination. On the day before the Big 4-0, I went for a long walk on the beach. I stood on the wet sand, facing the ocean, arms outstretched letting the salty sea breeze buffet me. I untied my ponytail of blonde curls and let them dance wildly in the wind. I twirled around, trying to shake loose the emotional tethers that were holding me back, and then did a pathetic cartwheel. That seemed to do the trick. Within a month, I was packing my bags for Paris. I had lined up a few travel-writing assignments. I said good-bye to my on-and-off boyfriend, who wished me well. I landed in Paris' sixth arrondissement, in a quintessentially romantic garret apartment in Saint-Germain-des-Prés, a block from Hemingway's hangout Les Deux Magots. Unromantically, my apartment was 77 steps above street level. A good workout for my thighs and tush that were straining the seams of my jeans with every croissant I ate.

The first week after I arrived, I met Nicole who worked part-time at an art gallery down the street from my building. We bonded over *café au lait* and pastries at the *boulangerie* next to the gallery. She told me about her gig in Giverny during the tourist season.

A major American Impressionist show was opening in Chicago later in the year and the editor at one of the magazines I wrote for wanted a piece about the American artists who had followed Monet to Giverny. When I told Nicole about the assignment, she insisted I come observe one of her sessions at the lodge. Her course is popular with American painting groups. The lure of the program is that her students have access to Monet's gardens after public-viewing hours. They're free to roam the grounds and set up their easels wherever they feel inspired, capturing the beauty of the gardens in early evening.

So there I was, on a modern-day pilgrimage to the village that had captivated a generation of artists a century ago.

Nicole was with her students in the studio behind the lodge. Alyce greeted me at the door, wide-eyed. "We've had quite a morning."

Nicole was consoling a woman whose painting had a huge smear across the middle. "You can re-work this area. I will show you how," Nicole assured her.

"I think I want to leave it – just as it is," the woman said cheerfully. "As a souvenir of the day."

"What happened?" I asked Alyce.

"We were in a field painting haystacks. A cow came up behind her and licked her canvas."

I stifled a giggle. "Everyone's a critic."

Nicole smiled at me. "Kate, what do you think? Should she leave it this way?"

"Absolutely," I said. "What a story."

Nicole turned to the group. "She's a writer. Of course, she would say that."

"It's an authentic *plein-air* experience." I picked up a course brochure from a table by the door. "Just like it says here."

Nicole laughed. I had written the copy for the brochure.

"Kate is right," Nicole told the group. "Painting *en plein air* – when you're on location, out in the open air – exposes you to nature in all its glorious forms. And some not so glorious." She turned to the woman whose painting had been cow-licked. "You had an Impressionist experience today."

I took some photos of the students working at their easels and then wandered back to the lodge to do some reading.

The lodge had an inviting main room off the entry hallway, with a large dining area that easily could accommodate a dozen guests. At the far end, a big comfy sofa and a few overstuffed chairs faced a stone fireplace. An old upright piano sat in the corner. Paintings of Giverny and the surrounding countryside covered the walls – samples of student work. Some were quite impressive.

The coffee table by the sofa was covered with art books. One had caught my eye the night before, about an artist named Theodore Robinson. I had read in the catalog for the upcoming Chicago exhibition that Robinson's work would be featured. He was one of the first American painters who had come to Giverny and was one of the few Monet had welcomed into his inner circle.

When Monet moved to Giverny in 1883, at the age of 42, he sought the solace of the countryside. He had been living in the Paris suburb of Poissy, which he detested. He was drawn to the pastoral landscapes of Normandy and its scenic coastline. Giverny had a charm of its own. It was a quiet village of 300 residents back then (about 500 now, in the off-season) – no more than a cluster of modest stone houses nestled against a hillside, bordered by farms and orchards.

Monet rented his now-famous pink stucco house known as Maison du Pressoir, named for an apple press nearby, on a property at the east end of the village. He purchased it in 1890 and lived there until his death, at the age of 86, in 1926.

He enjoyed the solitude of Giverny for only a few years before other artists, who had come to the Seine valley to paint *en plein air,* discovered picturesque Giverny. In 1887, several American painters spent the summer in Giverny, which soon became a mecca for other American artists eager to be part of the breakaway movement that Monet and other renegade French artists were championing at the time. Their fractured and fragmented depictions, which focused on the interplay of color and light, were a radical departure from established artistic conventions, causing one critic to derisively label their style "Impressionism."

Monet got so fed up with Giverny's American invasion that, in 1892, he threatened to leave the village. He stayed on, but kept to himself behind the walls of his sprawling gardens, allowing only invited friends and colleagues and a select few of the Americans in Giverny into his sanctum.

Robinson was one of the honored few. I knew from my research that his friendship with Monet had had a profound influence on his work. Robinson, who was in his mid-30s when he met Monet, had studied with well-known academic teachers of the day. But with Monet as his mentor, Robinson developed a style that set him apart as an American Impressionist painter.

As I paged through the coffee-table book, which contained many photos of Robinson's Giverny paintings, I was intrigued with his storytelling ability as an artist. Many of his paintings depicted local residents – especially women – as they went about their daily tasks: sewing, picking fruit, washing laundry in a stream, drawing water from a well.

One, in particular, was beautifully rendered. A woman in a ruffled summer dress sat at the end of a low stone bridge, with a book in her lap, gazing at the stream. I looked closer at the bridge. It was just like the one by the moulin.

∽

The afternoon turned gray and drizzly. The group had decided to continue working in the studio, but Alyce offered to take me to the gardens. She knew I was eager.

Alyce and Tom ran a well-known art school in Naples, Florida, and worked with Nicole as the U.S. coordinators for her Giverny program. Alyce and Tom were in residence at the lodge from late spring through fall and handled a lot of the day-to-day arrangements for the program, allowing Nicole to focus on the art course.

When Alyce and I arrived at the garden gate, the guards were ushering out the last of the day's visitors. One guard nodded at Alyce as we entered.

"I'm so happy to be with a VIP," I whispered to her.

"They know me by name. I'm here every day."

We followed a path that led to the bottom of the garden, which is named Le Clos Normand. Although the garden's rectangular beds are arranged in a grid, with paths between them, the overall effect of the plantings is chaotic. Late in the season, the beds appeared to be a wild tangle of flowers.

"The untamed look is intentional," Alyce told me. "Monet liked what he called a 'cottagey jungle.' He mixed wild flowers with herbs and exotic plants. He designed the planting scheme so that the garden would be in bloom throughout the season. He thought about color combinations and the height of the plants. He placed cool tones in shady spots and the more vibrant colors in full sun."

Under grey skies, the colors of the flowers were more subdued than I had seen in photographs of the gardens. But it was easy to see the painterly effect Monet had envisioned.

Vaulted trellises laden with roses arched over a wide pathway called the Grande Allée that led from the foot of the garden up to the house. The path itself had almost disappeared under a carpet of yellow and orange nasturtiums.

"There's a wonderful photo of Monet, with his long white beard and wide-brimmed hat, standing here in the Grande Allée the year before he died," Alyce said. "The scene then looks just the same as now, with nasturtiums crawling across the path. The caretakers today follow Monet's planting designs and his meticulous botanical journals. They still have records of his plant and seed orders. He knew a lot about horticulture and sought out plant experts."

In the late 1890s, Monet bought an adjacent property where he dug a basin for his lily pond and to fill it, diverted a stream called the Ru – the same stream that flows by the moulin. The problem was that Monet's two properties were separated by railway tracks and a dirt road. Traffic on the roadway created a lot of dust, which settled on the water lilies. Monet wanted them looking fresh so he instructed his gardeners to paddle out onto the pond every day and rinse them off.

Alyce led me to a tunnel – added during a major renovation project before the gardens opened to the public in 1980 – that goes under that same road and gives visitors access to the water garden.

The air was heavy with mist as we walked the path by the pond. A light rain began to fall. Alyce and I took cover on the Japanese bridge under its shelter of wisteria vines.

I was mesmerized by the tiny rippling circles on the pond's surface. The water lilies were smudges of pink and yellow on the watery canvas before us. An intricate spider's web, spun on the vines, glistened with silver droplets. A weeping willow swayed gently in the breeze. It was one of those pinch-me moments. For years I had gazed at Monet's paintings of this scene and now was experiencing its soul-stirring beauty for myself.

~

I had dinner that evening with the group at the lodge. Nicole employed a gourmet chef to cook for her students, so meals there were quite a treat. The chef's French country menu included recipes from Monet's own cooking journals: *poulet chasseur, légumes farcis* and *gigot d'agneau.* Dessert that night was to die for – *poires Hélène.* We played a game at the table, drawing pictures with our spoons in the dark chocolate sauce that remained in our dessert bowls. Very little sauce remained in mine – Ms. Piggy that I am – but I managed to sketch a convincing haystack. *Très* Monet.

Tom and Alyce offered to walk me back to the moulin. It was still raining, and as much as I appreciated their company, I didn't want them venturing out into the damp night. Tom was just getting over a nasty cold.

It was only 10 o'clock when I left the lodge, but the entire village seemed to be sound asleep. There was no moonlight to guide me, but shepherd-crook streetlights kept the shadows at bay.

It was a 10-minute walk to the moulin. I had no trouble opening the gate. I waved my arms as I crossed the courtyard to keep the floodlight on while I opened the front door.

Gérard had left the dining room light on and a note on the table, next to a hot water bottle: *I got the radiators working today. Your room should be toasty. Here's a hot water bottle. I hate cold sheets. Help yourself to whatever is in the fridge if you're wanting a midnight snack. See you in the morning. p.s. We'll try to be quieter. G*

Sweet. I wondered what had happened with his fiancée.

There was water in the electric kettle on the sideboard. I made quick work of filling the bottle and headed upstairs.

The room was toasty, as promised. I slid the bottle under the covers and pulled the curtains shut.

I paused for a moment under the vault of the ceiling and sang a verse of *Goodnight, My Someone* to my phantom.

Then I quickly put on my pajamas and tucked myself into my warm bed.

Sweet dreams, I whispered. I fell asleep to the sound of water spilling over the paddle wheel under the moulin.

2

The next morning, I slipped into jeans and my favorite baggy sweater and tied back my mop of curls, anxious to start the day.

I found another note from Gérard on the dining table: *Out for a bit. Coffee in pitcher. Treats in basket. G*

Gérard had the stylized handwriting of an architect – angular letters that looked like they'd been written along the edge of a ruler. So unlike my loopy scroll that filled my journals.

Next to the note, Gérard had left a tourist-bureau map of the village. He had circled the American Impressionist museum and, in his precise script, had written "Pierre Gaston" in the margin, along with a phone number. Gérard had told me Pierre was a friend who worked as a curator at the museum and would be happy to talk with me about my article.

I poured myself some coffee from the thermal pitcher on the buffet and peeked under the napkin covering the basket. A selection of amazing pastries by Henri. I couldn't resist a *sacristan,* a twisted pastry strip encrusted with caramelized sugar and almonds. I wanted to meet Henri and ask him to marry me.

It was a sunny morning, so I decided to have my breakfast *en plein air* and went out to the patio behind the moulin. Coco, who had been napping in a sunny patch on the flagstones, came to greet me as I sat down. She looked longingly at the *sacristan.*

"Are you allowed to have this?" I asked her. Her eyes seemed to say *yes,* so I gave her a tiny piece. She gobbled it up and waited for another.

"You French girls have to watch your waistline," I told her. I scratched her head as she rested her chin on my knee. I had just made a new friend.

From the moulin's patio, I could see round bales of hay in a field with a stand of poplar trees along the horizon – a scene Monet may have painted, except that his haystacks looked like thatched huts.

I sipped my coffee, feeling the sun on my face. A perfect morning to photograph the gardens. The tour buses wouldn't be rolling in for another couple of hours, so I could get some good shots without the crowds.

Coco jumped up as the front door opened. Gérard called out, "Hel-lo!" She ran to greet him.

"Hi! I'm out on the patio."

Gérard appeared at the dining room's French doors. "Good morning." He had a grin that could light up a room. "Have you two ladies been keeping each other company?"

"We have – come join us."

"I'll grab some coffee. Would you like a fresh cup?"

"I'd love some."

Gérard returned with coffee and the pastry basket. "Did you try these?" he asked, lifting the napkin.

"Yes, and I forced myself to leave the basket in the dining room."

"*Mais non* – it belongs out here. A croissant, perhaps? *Peut-être?*"

"*Peut-être.*"

"Good. Me, too. Let me get the jam."

I laughed when he returned with the jar, looking like a ravenous kid ready to attack an after-school snack.

"Hungry?" I asked.

"You work up an appetite doing manual labor."

"And what have you been laboring at this morning?"

"I was at the lumber yard, getting some planks milled. I want to get a new roof on the gatehouse before winter."

The gatehouse was in shambles. Half the roof shingles were missing, exposing the rafters in places. The exterior walls were crumbling with gaping holes where the windows had been.

"That'll be a big project, " I said.

"I know it looks like a wreck, but it's structurally sound. It's fascinating to see the construction methods and the materials they used back then. They built it for the ages."

"How old is this place?"

"The original section of the moulin was built in 1761," he said, pointing at the stone structure above the water wheel. "Many changes were made over the years. The tower is part of the original building, but the gatehouse was probably added later. You'll see it in one of the paintings at the museum."

"Really?"

"The little bridge – the one across the road – is in the foreground. Behind that, you see the stone wall and the gatehouse, which is a creamy stucco with pale green shutters in the painting."

"Who's the artist?"

"Theodore Robinson. He painted a lot of scenes around the moulin."

"I've been reading about him. He painted a woman sitting by a bridge – was it this bridge here?"

Gérard nodded. "You can't see the moulin in that painting. But it's definitely this bridge. There's an interesting story about Robinson. He suffered from asthma and couldn't spend all day in the field painting. So he worked from photographs he took – quite good ones – of people and scenes around Giverny. You'll see a collection of his photos at the museum. There's a wonderful one of women washing clothes in the stream, down by the bridge, with the gate of the moulin in the background. He photographed women a lot. He seemed to have an eye for the ladies…"

Just then, a horn honked at the front gate.

Gérard looked at his watch. "That was fast. It's my lumber delivery." He took a swig of his coffee as he stood up. "To be continued. Maybe this evening, if you're not busy. We could have dinner at the Baudy."

"I'd love to. I haven't been there yet."

"Okay, I'll meet you here at 7 and we can walk up together."

"Sounds good."

"Sorry to rush off." Gérard disappeared, with Coco at his heels.

I gathered up my gear and called Pierre at the museum. He was cordial and suggested we meet the next morning.

Gérard and the driver of the lumber truck were off-loading sheets of plywood in the courtyard as I headed out. They were laughing about something. Gérard really seemed to be in his element. He wasn't lord of the manor, overseeing the heavy lifting. He had work gloves on, sleeves rolled up, putting muscle into rebuilding the moulin.

He waved as I walked across the courtyard. I waved back, happy that I would be seeing him later. I had so many questions I wanted to ask him about what it was like growing up here. Nicole had told me that several local families had lived in Giverny for more than 200 years. She had a friend in Giverny whose mother had worked as a housekeeper for one of Monet's stepdaughters. It was incredible to me that there were people living in Giverny who knew of him through his children. One degree of separation.

I arrived at the gardens ahead of the tour groups and followed the route that Alyce had taken. The visual effect of the flowerbeds in sunlight was entirely different from the overcast day before. The colors were vibrant – red, yellow, orange, lavender and pink – and looked like splotches of paint on a palette. I walked along the paths between the beds, with exuberant sprays of cosmos and giant sunflowers towering over me. Dazzling clusters of dahlias, with their spidery petals, looked like the floral equivalent of fireworks.

I found my way to the tunnel leading to the lily pond and took the path to the Japanese bridge. A few puffy white clouds, against the cornflower-blue sky, reflected on the water's surface. The wispy willow branches dangled above the pond. The lily pads seemed to float on the mirrored image of the trees, sky and clouds.

Monet immortalized his lily pond in some 250 paintings, including the iconic *Nymphéas* panels that are now displayed at the Musée de l'Orangerie in Paris. In the early 1920s, Monet helped the Louvre's head architect Camille Lefèvre design the museum's two exhibit rooms for the eight water-lily murals. The canvases are mounted on curved walls, giving the illusion of a third dimension, under diffused natural light. Monet painted the panels in a specially designed studio, adjacent to his house in Giverny. The space is now used as the tourist gift shop.

Tour groups were arriving as I headed to the exit, via the shop. On a postcard rack, I saw a photo, dated 1922, of Monet standing in the same room when it was his studio. Some of the water-lily canvases line the walls. The high, sloped ceiling looks much the same as it does today – its skylights draped with light-filtering fabric, strung on pulley-operated cables. In the photo, the studio is empty except for a worn overstuffed sofa, a wooden armchair and an end table. Monet, with his long white beard, stands by the table, smoking a cigarette.

A cushy sofa in the gift shop, similar to the one in the photo, beckoned me. I sat down with a book of vintage postcard photos of Giverny, including two of the moulin. One photo is of a snowy scene showing American painter

Stanton Young, who bought and refurbished the moulin in the early 1900s, standing on the railway tracks that ran by the moulin, with the gatehouse behind him. The moulin's tower and the large arched window of my room are visible through the bare snow-dusted branches of the trees.

~

I found Nicole and a few of her students at a café across the street from the gardens.

"Where have you been?" Nicole asked, as I pulled up a chair. Her long auburn hair caught the sunlight. She had shed her Parisian haute-couture style in favor of an off-the-shoulder peasant top over fashionably ripped jeans. Nicole was the epitome of French chic and up on all the latest catwalk trends. She had been threatening to take me clothes shopping, but I was still stubbornly clinging to my California dress code – naturally faded jeans, tank tops and flip-flops.

"Time traveling," I said. I showed her the book of vintage postcards, one of my many book purchases that morning. "Except for the Victorian outfits these people are wearing, not much has changed here."

"That's the beauty of it. You feel like you're in another era. Have you been to the museum yet? We're going there on a tour after lunch. You're welcome to join us."

"Perfect. Tomorrow I'm seeing Monsieur Gaston, the curator Gérard knows. I need to do my homework."

"Nice of Gérard to suggest that. How he is?"

"He's been the perfect host."

"I'm glad. He seemed so unhappy when he came back to Giverny. I don't know what happened in London." Nicole lit a cigarette. "It seems his friend Julie is involved somehow."

"The decorator?"

"He's told you about her?"

"Not really. He mentioned her when we were talking about the furnishings. Do you know her?"

"I met her once, in Paris last spring. She and Gérard came to an opening at the gallery. Apparently, she's at the moulin a lot." A puff of smoke escaped Nicole's frosted pink lips as she laughed. "The old grannies in the village love to gossip."

～

The art museum in Giverny would undergo changes in the years to come. But at the time of my first visit there, it held a treasure trove of paintings by the American artists who came to Giverny in the late 1800s – many of them in residence or frequent visitors there until the outbreak of World War I.

The museum, then known as the Musée d'Art Américain Giverny, was created in 1992 by American industrialist Daniel J. Terra, a passionate collector of American Impressionist art. As much as my vintage-postcard book had taken me on a visual tour of old Giverny, the paintings of the Terra Foundation collection provided another portal into the world of Giverny's artist colony.

Most of the American Impressionist artists were new to me, but I instantly loved their work. A scene of a deserted moonlit

Giverny street by Thomas Buford Meteyard reminded me of my late-night walks from the lodge to the moulin. Dawson Dawson-Watson captured the idyllic charm of the village's meandering lanes, bordered by garden walls, clumps of wild-flowers and the front stoops of cottages.

Giverny's haystacks were a favorite subject, obviously influenced by Monet's extensive studies of them in chang-ing weather and seasons. John Leslie Breck produced a series of 15 haystack paintings called *Studies of an Autumn Day*, imitating Monet's technique of observing the meta-morphosis of a single scene in what appears to be the span of a day, from daybreak to twilight.

It was interesting to see how the American painters in Giverny moved away from their academic training and the classical tenets of realism, adopting the brighter pal-ette and free-form brushwork of their French Impressionist peers. Some were more progressive and experimental than others. I especially liked the bold, luminous paintings of Frederick Carl Frieseke, who in later years painted nudes in a secluded garden at the edge of the village. Although nude models were common in the studios of Paris, it was pushing the limits of decorum to have nudity on display in a garden, no matter how secluded.

At the heart of the museum's collection were Robin-son's paintings. The one Gérard had told me about, with the moulin's gatehouse in the background, shows a man named Père Trognon crossing the stream on horseback, with his daughter watching from the bridge.

The museum docent who led our group that after-noon told us the story of Robinson's painting *The Wedding*

March, a lovely depiction of the wedding procession of fellow American artist Theodore Butler and his new bride, Monet's stepdaughter Suzanne Hoschedé.

"It's not clear whether the man escorting the veiled bride is Theodore Butler – or Monet," our guide Louise noted. "The wedding party processes from the *mairie,* the town hall in Giverny where the civil ceremony took place, to the village church. As you have seen, the *mairie* still exists today – it's across the street from the lodge where you're staying. But it no longer has pink stucco, as you see here, which was popular in Monet's time." Louise raised an already dramatically arched eyebrow. "Only four days earlier, Monet married Suzanne's mother. Monet and Madame Hoschedé had been living together – quite a scandal in those days – but finally her husband passed away, making their marriage possible."

Nicole, standing next to Louise, smiled at the group. "Just a footnote – Suzanne died seven years later. Her grieving husband married her sister, Marthe, the following year. And you Americans think our French men behave badly?"

Tom laughed. "He was lonely and she was willing. What's so bad about that?" Alyce gave him a playful poke in the ribs.

Louise led us to another gallery where some of Robinson's photographs were on display.

"Robinson was an accomplished photographer and documented village life in Giverny, capturing local residents doing mundane daily chores." She pointed to the photo Gérard had told me about, of women washing clothes in the stream by the bridge at the moulin. It was a study for a painting Robinson called *Gossips.*

Louise turned to another photograph of a woman sewing, sitting on a chair in a walled garden. "But this is not a Giverny girl. Her name is Marie. We don't know her last name or much else about her, except that she was a Parisian model and a close friend of Robinson's who spent time with him here in Giverny. She appears in many of his paintings. Her features are distinct as you can see – her upturned nose and protruding upper lip."

I raised my hand. "Is she the woman sitting by the bridge at the moulin, in another of his paintings?"

"Yes. That's a famous Robinson painting called *La Débâcle* – named for the book of that title by Émile Zola that she's holding. The woman in that picture is definitely the mysterious Marie."

~

I left the group after the museum tour, happy to go back to the moulin and put my feet up.

Gérard was out, but Coco was happy to see me. I had picked up a bottle of Bourgogne *rouge* at a little grocery store in the village. I poured a glass and went out to the patio. It felt good to stretch out on a chaise. I watched the clouds float across the sky. The season was changing. There was a nip in the air as the sun sank behind the trees. Leaves rustled in the breeze. I watched a swirl of them dance overhead…

The next sound I heard was a man softly saying my name. I opened my eyes to see Gérard smiling down at me.

"Good morning," he said.

I suddenly was wide-awake. "What time is it?"

"You slept all night out here. I covered you with a pile of blankets so you wouldn't freeze."

"Seriously…" I looked at my watch. It said 6:30. "Ohhh." I yawned and stretched. "Did you just get back?"

"A little while ago. You looked so peaceful. I didn't want to disturb you. Did you have a good day?"

"Wonderful."

"You can tell me all about it at dinner."

"Let me go freshen up."

It didn't take me long. Tunic sweater over black leggings, with a jean jacket. Funky earrings and a little lipstick. Curls loose, with a touch of mousse. Complete transformation. Or at least a good attempt.

Gérard seemed impressed. "Lovely," he said, as I came down the stairs. "In ten minutes. *Mon dieu*. I've never known a woman who could get ready that fast."

I smiled at him. "I have many talents."

As we walked up the lane from the moulin, Gérard told me about the famous neighbors from long ago. We passed a three-story pink-stucco house appropriately called La Maison Rose that had been rented by Czech painter Václav Radimský. Later, the house became an inn, where actors, writers and painters from Paris congregated on weekends. Dancer Isadora Duncan had been a regular.

"It was a hideaway for lovers." Gérard smiled. "Can you imagine what went on there. Couples naked in the bushes. Isadora dancing in the garden."

I laughed. "You have a fertile imagination."

"Giverny was a lively place back then, especially in the summer. My grandfather grew up here during Monet's time and vividly remembers the American artists. Most of them were young bachelors, enjoying the bohemian life. They had come to Paris to study, show their work, build their reputations. But an artist's life in Paris wasn't easy. Here, they felt at home, thanks to Madame Baudy. She really took care of them. They were like kids at camp." Gérard chuckled. "With lots of adult activities."

Angélina Baudy and her husband Lucien had the good business sense to embrace their foreign visitors. They converted what originally was a small grocery store and café into a *pension*, with 20 bedrooms, a dining room, three painting studios, a billiard room and a ballroom. They even built two tennis courts to please their American guests. Although tennis was practically unknown in France at the time, the courts at the Hôtel Baudy drew many curious spectators. Stanton Young had taken charge of the tennis-court construction project.

Madame Baudy was an accommodating hostess. She expanded her menu of Normandy dishes to include Boston baked beans, porridge and cornflakes. She imported five brands of whiskey, an exotic drink in France at the time. Room-and-board was only four cents a night – and that included unlimited red wine.

Villagers referred to the Baudy as the "American Painters Hotel," but it became a cosmopolitan meeting place. Art dealers and collectors came to Giverny to buy directly from the artists. The dining room of the Baudy had the look of a makeshift gallery, its walls crowded with paintings. Madame Baudy made sure her artists never ran out of paints and canvases – she became a vendor for the Paris art-supply company Lefebvre-Foinet.

Although the Hôtel Baudy no longer offers overnight lodging, it is still a popular café-restaurant where tourists and artists gather. The dining room walls are decorated with paintings of local artists. Outdoor dining is available across the street under the shade of linden trees, overlooking an open field where the tennis courts used to be.

Candles were lit at the tables in the dining room when Gérard and I arrived. We were the first guests of the evening. The barman seated us by a window and handed us a menu of hearty Normandy dishes: *cuisse de canard, brochette d'agneau* and *noix d'entrecôte.* No sign of baked beans. But on the children's menu – chicken nuggets.

I still had my book of vintage postcards in my bag and showed it to Gérard. There were several photos of the Baudy, its façade virtually unchanged.

"Look at this," Gérard said, pointing to a photo of the dining room. "We're sitting right here." He glanced around the room. "The ceramic stove is the same. The doors, wainscoting, moldings – same."

I showed him the photos of the moulin. He had never seen the one of Stanton Young standing by the gatehouse in the snow.

"Interesting – you can see the arched window of your room. This is the earliest photo I've seen of that window." Gérard chuckled as he read the photo caption. "It says here that American painter Stanton Young turned the moulin into *un ravissant cottage américain.*"

"Some cottage."

"Young's renovations were extensive," Gérard told me. "He added that big window and used your room as a painting studio. But according to local lore, your room was used as a studio even before Young bought the place." He smiled. "Can you guess who our famous artist-in-residence was?"

I smiled. "Truly?"

"*Vraiment*." Gérard lifted his wine glass. "Here's to Theodore Robinson."

My phantom.

~

I was feeling warmed and mellowed by the bottle of wine we had shared at dinner. We had laughed a lot, sharing funny stories about adapting to life in a foreign country.

I didn't ask why he had returned to Giverny. But as we walked back to the moulin, Gérard opened the door a crack when he asked why I had left California.

"I felt restless. I wanted to travel. I didn't have anything tying me down. I'm a writer – I can do my work anywhere. Why not?"

"Have you ever been married – if I may ask."

"No. You?"

"I came close about a year ago."

"Did you get cold feet?" I asked.

Gérard was quiet for a moment. "I had a very warm heart. But yes, in the end, she gave me cold feet."

We walked in silence for a bit.

It was a beautiful clear night. The moon was rising above the silhouettes of the poplars along the banks of the Ru.

"I'm lucky to have this place," he said. "I know that. It's good to have a home port."

"Will you stay?"

"Probably not. I don't think about what next too much. The moulin has been my focus for the past year. That's been good for me."

"*Busy hands are happy hands* – my grandmother used to say that."

He looked at me. "Are you happy in your new life here?"

"Very. I'm so glad I did this."

"It takes courage."

"I don't feel especially brave. It's not like I've moved to a war zone."

"No, but it takes a lot of inner strength to know what you want and go after it, especially when you're leaving behind family, friends and everything that's familiar to you."

"Some days I get a little homesick, I must admit."

"What do you miss most?"

"Tacos and guacamole."

Gérard laughed. "I know of a good Mexican restaurant in Paris. Next time I'm in the city, I'll take you there."

"Deal."

∿

As I undressed for bed, I heard the *chouette*. I opened a window and listened to her soulful cries.

In the field behind the moulin, the moon had turned the tassels of cornstalks a shimmering gold. Clouds raced across the sky, their shadows chasing each other across the landscape. The cool damp air sent a chill through me.

I closed the window and took a blanket from the foot of the bed. I wrapped myself tight and stood at the center of the room, looking up at the peak of the vaulted ceiling.

"I know your name," I whispered.

And then for some strange reason, my eyes filled with tears as I sang to him.

3

Pierre Gaston was in his office at the museum when I arrived the next morning. He was on the phone, but motioned for me to take a seat.

"That won't be possible," he said adamantly. "It will take a week to crate the painting and deliver it to customs. And then there's the paperwork. Even with express delivery, it will be at least two weeks before it arrives."

He kept shaking his head as he paced around the room, listening to the person at the other end. "I will try my best. But these things can't be rushed. *Oui*…okay…*au revoir*."

Pierre clicked off. "*Mon dieu*. Such an unreasonable woman. She demands the moon."

He excused himself for a moment to speak to his secretary in the outer office. I heard him say, in French, "Call Margot Mallery and apologize to her for the short notice. Confirm the details with the shipping company."

The name Mallery got my attention. Over breakfast that morning, Gérard had invited me to a party that evening at the home of a woman named Mallery. He said she was an art collector.

Pierre reappeared, but looked distracted. "So Gérard tells me you're writing an article about the Americans. What do you need from me?"

Not the most gracious opening, but I succinctly outlined the premise of the article, explaining that I would be focusing on the stories of the artists who would be featured in the Chicago exhibition – Theodore Robinson, John Leslie Breck, Guy Rose, Frederick Carl Frieseke, Lilla Cabot Perry, Willard Leroy Metcalf, Theodore Butler, and Mary and Frederick MacMonnies.

Pierre reached for a booklet on the credenza behind his desk. "This is a helpful guide, with a map marked with important locations in Giverny during that time – where the artists lived, scenes they painted."

I flipped through the pages and saw Robinson's *La Débâcle*. "Gérard seems to think that Robinson used the moulin as his studio."

"Some say that. But I don't know if there's truth to it. Robinson certainly painted many scenes near the moulin."

"I was here yesterday and our guide told us about Marie – the mystery model. What do you know about her?"

"Pfffff…" He seemed to dismiss the question with a puff of air. "She's a mystery."

"There's no record of her? Correspondence?"

"Why does she interest you?" I could sense his impatience.

"Apparently, she was his favorite model and spent a lot of time in Giverny. What was their story?"

"You want to write about the gossip of Giverny? Or the art?"

"Both. Giverny was a thriving artists' colony where life and art were intertwined."

"I can only help you with the art. Yes, she appears in many of his paintings. But no one knows her full name or what happened to her after he died."

"I've read that Robinson kept detailed journals. Do you have any of his diaries or correspondence here at the museum?"

"No, we have nothing like that."

"What do you know about his relationship with Monet?"

"They were friends. Monet liked him because he was older than the rest of the Americans who came here. Robinson had academic training, with a body of work and experience. He wasn't a novice who had come to copy Monet."

Pierre glanced at his watch. I took that as a signal that my time was up and thanked him for chatting with me, although I hadn't gotten much from our brief session.

"I'm sorry – today is very busy for me. We are preparing to ship several paintings for the Chicago exhibition. If you need more information, you may contact me." He gave me his card and escorted me to the outer office.

Pierre might be a useful contact at some point, I thought. But not that day.

I wandered through the galleries again and lingered at the photo of Marie. I took the vintage-postcard book from my bag and found the photo of the Baudy dining room that Gérard and I had looked at the night before.

There, on the dining room wall, was a painting of Marie, inspired by the same photograph.

~

It's impossible to get lost in Giverny. Along the main street, aptly named Rue Claude Monet, is the Sainte Radégonde church and the adjacent cemetery where Monet is buried. The street passes the Hôtel Baudy and a cluster of artist studios and shops at the heart of the village. Farther on, it actually runs along the backside of Monet's house, which sits a few feet from the curb. It's no wonder Monet guarded his privacy. His bedroom window is in plain view, just above the garden wall that separates the property from the street.

Next door to Monet's compound is a property called *Le Hameau* – The Hamlet – which had been the summer home of American painter Lilla Cabot Perry, who was from a prominent Boston family and whose personal friends included Louisa May Alcott and Ralph Waldo Emerson. She was instrumental in promoting the Impressionist movement in the United States, where she organized private and public exhibitions of her compatriots' paintings. Like Robinson, Perry was a friend of Monet's. When she met him in 1889, she wrote to friends in the States of "a very great artist only beginning to be known, whose pictures could be bought from his studio in Giverny for the sum of $500."

Following the map in the guidebook Pierre had given me, I turned down a street, just west of Monet's house, called Rue du Pressoir and within a few steps I saw "*Le Hameau*" in wrought-iron letters on a garden wall, next to an open gate. I couldn't resist.

I stepped inside the garden enclosure and felt transported to another day long ago.

It was summer and there was a tea party in the garden. The women wore long, elegant dresses. One, in a wide-brimmed hat, stole a glance at me. Her friend, pouring tea at the table, didn't notice me as I inhaled the perfume of white lilies that lined the path in front of the cottage, covered with vines and roses that climbed over mint-green shutters and latticework.

It was as if I were standing in a painting by Carl Frederick Frieseke called *Lilies*, which I had seen at the museum the day before. The floral border, the rambling vines, even the color of the shutters and the latticework were the same. *Lilies* and another Frieseke painting called *Tea Time in a Giverny Garden* – both painted at *Le Hameau* – were inspiration for the 1994 restoration of the cottage, which became an art study center for the Terra Foundation.

I followed the map through the village. Madame Baudy's stone house, with vines encircling its distinctive round front window, sits at the curve of the road leading to the lodge and the *mairie*. The house has belonged to the Baudy family since the early 19th century and is now a B&B, run by Angélina's descendants. In the early days of the art colony, the house served as an annex to the hotel for Madame Baudy's favorite guests – including Robinson.

At the western end of the village, beyond the church, a 17ᵗʰ- century priory known as Le Prieuré, became a private enclave for friends of American artists Mary and Frederick MacMonnies, who purchased the property in the early 1900s. Le Prieuré's three-acre garden – with its shaded walkways, fruit trees, flowerbeds and reflecting pools – was the site of summer parties, theatrical events and musical evenings. The garden's high walls kept "the vulgar out," according to one artist. Reputedly, the politics and mores at the "MacMonastery," as it was fondly nicknamed, were liberal and loose.

I ended up back at the Hôtel Baudy, on the shaded terrace overlooking what had been the tennis courts, and enjoyed a delicious lunch of quiche Lorraine and for dessert, an apple tart smothered with *crème Chantilly*.

At one point, a woman who looked a bit like Helen Mirren walked past with a full-grown sheep on a leash. I did a double take. This wasn't a little lamb. It was a large, but gentle beast taking the local Ms. Bo Peep for a stroll.

After lunch, I explored the Baudy's back garden, through its labyrinth of pathways that climb the hillside behind the hotel. Perennials and rose bushes planted years ago are now part of a natural landscape, bordered by enormous trees on the ridgeline of the hill. Stone steps, nearly overgrown with summer sage and sprawling clumps of cranesbill geraniums, led me to secluded nooks, hidden by dense shrubs and vine-covered archways. I wondered if Theodore and Marie used to come here.

One of the Baudy's original painting studios, built in 1887, remains in the garden. The studio's interior – with an unfinished canvas still on its easel – looks as though the artist just left for lunch. A brush lies on a palette next to a pail of blue paint. The Baudy's studios were havens for painters during inclement weather and provided a private location for nude studies. The models were brought in from Paris, of course – what a *scandale* it would have been for village girls to pose.

A framed vintage photo on a wall of the studio made me smile. Three male artists – one with his feet propped up on a stool – appear to be taking a break, with their naked female model sitting primly, legs crossed, on an upholstered chair.

~

That evening, I was in for a surprise – more than one, actually.

Gérard hadn't really said much about Madame Mallery, except that she was an art collector who had connections with Giverny's Impressionist museum.

"She has these *soirées* every so often for museum patrons and Giverny's art crowd," he had told me at breakfast. "She lives in Paris and has a country house not far from here."

It was just getting dark as we pulled through the front gate of the Mallery estate, known as *Les Marguerites*. I let out a little gasp. "You call this a country house?"

"Well, it's a house in the country," Gérard said matter-of-factly.

"It's more like a chateau."

The Mallery mansion sat on a bluff overlooking the Seine. In twilight, with a few bright stars twinkling overhead and its turret silhouetted against the cobalt sky, it looked like it belonged on the cover of a romance novel.

"It's not *exactly* Versailles." Gérard clearly was enjoying my first surprise of the evening.

"Close enough," I said, quickly assessing my outfit. Simple black dress accessorized with a hand-painted silk scarf – my only splurge purchase since my arrival in Paris. Same funky earrings from the night before. "Should I have worn a gown and my powdered wig?"

"You look lovely – and very arty. You'll fit right in." He smiled at me. "I agonized over my outfit, I'll have you know."

Gérard looked very British in his Harris tweed jacket. "Quite dapper, I must say." As if he needed my assurance.

"I've been told I scrub up pretty well." He laughed. "But it's not so easy these days."

We parked in front of the house, in the circular driveway that was already crowded with cars. The party was in full swing.

A butler greeted us at the door and within moments, a waiter had served us champagne.

It was one of those evenings when, at every turn, there was an interesting character – a flamboyant artist, a dreamy poet, a Paris gallery owner, even a medieval-manuscript conservator. And then there were the moneymen, impeccably groomed still sporting summer tans from the Riviera, and their bejeweled wives – one who carried her tiny curly-furred Fifi in her Chanel shoulder bag.

Gérard was very attentive, making introductions. At one point, when we were out of everyone's earshot, I whispered, "How do you know Madame Mallery?"

"I did some design work for her when she was renovating this place. Her son is a friend of mine." He flagged a waiter and traded in our empty champagne glasses for a second round. "Come. Let me show you something."

We walked out onto a terrace facing the bluff. Gérard pointed to the back of the house, where an immense conservatory had been added. "For her prize orchid collection," he told me.

"You designed that?"

Gérard nodded. "She wanted something that looked English Victorian. That's not the style of the house. But we talked about her vision, and she was open to my suggestions."

"It's beautiful."

The conservatory's amber interior light gave the glass-paneled walls a surreal iridescence, framed by the elegant tracing of the decorative mullions. There was a weight to the design that made it feel anchored and part of the house, not a gothic gingerbread annex.

"I'm happy with how it turned out. Margot is an interesting woman. I don't know her background, but her husband was a well-known attorney who handled art forgery cases. That was his specialty. He represented museums around the world and had a huge reputation. Very successful. Margot spent their money wisely on art. The Mallery collection is rumored to be extensive and quite valuable."

"Rumored?"

"Their paintings apparently aren't seen very often. That's the trouble with priceless art. It's an insurance and security nightmare."

"Have they donated pieces to the museum?"

"A few. The Mallerys put a lot of money into that museum. He died a few years ago, but she's on the board and very influential."

We could hear a woman's voice rising above the din inside the house.

"That will be Margot," Gérard said, gently putting a hand at my back as we returned to the party.

I'll never forget that moment: my first glimpse of Madame Mallery, as I always addressed her. Apparently, this was her habit as a party hostess, to make a late appearance after holding court for her VIP guests elsewhere in the house. As she stood on the grand staircase in the galleried foyer that night, with a glass of champagne in hand, she seemed larger than life, exuding an air of sophistication and well-practiced charm. She wore a form-fitting red dress – vintage Valentino, someone next to me whispered – that showed off a shapely figure for her age (mid-70s, according to Gérard).

With a grand sweeping gesture to the crowd of guests in the foyer, she welcomed us to *Les Marguerites*. She had great poise and presence as she breathlessly told us about a recent acquisition by the museum. She also informed us that several pieces in the museum's collection would be traveling to the American Impressionist exhibition in Chicago. She raised her glass – instructing the waiters to be certain everyone could join her in a toast.

"Ici!" She pointed to a small group at the foot of the stairs who were empty-handed. "This will not do." She theatrically improvised with a look of feigned chagrin, to the amusement of her audience.

The serving staff was very efficient. We raised our glasses high as she saluted us with wishes of good health, long friendships and *moments d'enchantement romantique.*

Gérard and I clinked glasses. He winked at me. "Welcome to the House of Margot."

Madame Mallery made her way through the crowd, embracing guests and making small talk. She spied Gérard and quickly maneuvered her way to us.

"So delighted to see you, Gérard." She kissed him on both cheeks. "My orchids are so happy because of you. And so am I."

Gérard smiled at her. "I'm pleased to hear that."

"How is the work going at the moulin? I hear you've had some challenges there."

"Nothing insurmountable. But I've put a lot of sweat equity into that place."

"How was your first season?"

"I inched into the black this fall. That was my most-optimistic projection, so I'm happy. Weary, but happy."

Madame Mallery then fixed her eyes on me.

"I'd like you to meet Kate Morgan," Gérard said. "She's a magazine writer from California – now living in Paris – who's doing an article about Giverny's American Impressionists."

"What magazine will your article appear in?" she asked me, skipping pleasantries.

"*ARTnews*," I replied.

"I know it well." She seemed faintly impressed.

From behind me, a man cleared his throat. I turned to see Pierre Gaston.

"*Bonsoir, mademoiselle*," he said politely to me and then greeted Gérard with a handshake. "Good to see you, Gérard."

"Likewise, Pierre."

On our drive from Giverny, I had told Gérard that I had seen Pierre that morning, but hadn't mentioned that our meeting had been hasty or that Pierre had seemed preoccupied and impatient.

Pierre smiled at me, putting on a different face than he had that morning. "Have you told Madame Mallery about your article research?" He turned to her. "Kate had some interesting questions for me today. She was asking me about Robinson and his mystery model, Marie."

Madame Mallery suddenly was very interested in what I had to say.

"Gérard and I had been talking about Robinson's paintings of the moulin. I'm especially taken with his rendering of the woman sitting by the bridge…"

"*La Débâcle,*" Madame Mallery interjected.

"Yes. I understand the woman in the painting was one of Robinson's favorite models. I saw a photograph of her at the museum."

Madame Mallery shrugged. "He photographed many women in Giverny."

"But she was not from Giverny – she was Parisian, yes?"

"Very little is known about her. She's insignificant, really," she said. "Unfortunately, Robinson died at a young age – he was only 43 – and never gained the attention or acclaim of some of his peers. In the grand scheme of things, he's a *minor* artist."

That surprised me. "From what I've read, he ranked second only to Mary Cassatt among the American Impressionists."

"My dear, of course you're entitled to your opinion," Madame Mallery said dismissively. "But I would suggest you expand your research."

I felt myself stiffen. "He's a featured artist in the Chicago exhibition."

"One of *many* who were far more talented than he," she said pointedly.

With that, she took Pierre's arm. "Don't you have someone you want me to meet?" she asked him.

She smiled at Gérard. "Come over someday soon and see the orchids."

Pierre whisked her away, through a crush of admirers.

"Wow," I said under my breath. "What just happened?"

Gérard looked puzzled. "I don't know. How was your meeting today with Pierre – did things go well?"

"Not exactly," I admitted.

On the ride back to the moulin, I told Gérard about how Pierre had bristled at my questions about Marie and seemed to think I was more interested in Giverny's social scene than its artwork.

"To me, that's what makes Giverny's history so fascinating. This place is filled with stories and characters and romance and scandal." I smiled at Gérard. "And the paintings are wonderful, too."

He laughed. "Don't worry about Pierre. He can be a bit off-putting. And Margot – well, she can flatten you with arrogance. Don't let them bowl you over."

"I'm sorry if I've embarrassed you."

"Hardly." He grinned. "*I've* been invited to see the orchids."

We both laughed. Gérard reached over and squeezed my hand. *That* was the nicest surprise of the evening.

4

On my last day in Giverny, I had one more place I wanted to visit – the secluded garden at *Le Vivier*, the Fish-pond, where nude women posed *en plein air* for Frieseke and fellow American painters including Lawton Parker, Richard E. Miller and Louis Ritman. The models luxuri-ated on sun-dappled linens or were depicted shedding their clothes before taking a dip in the pond. Ironically, the pond has a somewhat sacred past. It was where the monks of ancient Giverny used to breed fish.

At breakfast, I showed Gérard the map in the guide-book Pierre had given me. *Le Vivier* appeared to be near the moulin.

"I'll take you there. I've got the key to the place," he said. "The owners live in Paris and have asked me to keep an eye on things."

Le Vivier is situated on the banks of the Ru. The Normandy-style cottage, barely visible from the main road, is accessed by a footbridge next to a brick-and-timber washhouse where women used to gather to do laundry in the stream.

We walked around to the side of the house. A high stone wall concealed the garden. Gérard unlocked the wooden garden gate.

The property had been neglected, but it was still possible to see its original beauty. In a way, the pond was a mini version of Monet's. An arched stone bridge crossed one end of it. A white wooden pergola sat on top of the bridge, its pillars supported by stone supports carved with the bearded faces of kingly men.

Gérard looked at the murky water of the pond. "The guy who bought this place accidentally killed all the fish when he was renovating the house. Slowly, they're coming back. Look there..." He pointed to a huge carp that was lurking under a lily pad. "They love to eat frogs." He pretended to snatch a fly out of the air, a few inches from my nose, which made me jump.

"You're bad." I couldn't help but laugh.

"Don't dangle your toes in the water."

We sat under the shade of a willow. Gérard lay back on the grass. "Did you bring your guidebook?" he asked, knowing I had. "Read to me."

I flipped to the chapter about the paintings from *Le Vivier*.

"As we know, Frederick Carl Frieseke used this location for his outdoor nude studies. He was from Owosso, Michigan," I noted.

"Where's that?" Gérard chewed on a blade of grass, lying comfortably with his hands behind his head.

"Michigan is considered Midwest. But it's actually north – it borders Canada – and its western border is Lake Michigan. I have no idea where Owosso is."

"Sounds like Indian territory."

"I think Frieseke was of German descent, not Indian."

"You're probably right. Continue."

"So it says here he married an American woman named Sadie, from Pittsburgh, who often was his model." I looked closer at the color prints of Frieseke's nudes. "Surely, she didn't pose naked for him."

"Why not?"

"She never would have been able to go back to Pittsburgh."

Gérard laughed. I showed him a photo in the book of a naked woman, with alabaster skin and perky breasts with rose-colored nipples. Her red pubic hair matched the hair on her head.

"Hmm," Gérard said. "A natural red-head. You don't see many of those around here." He smiled slyly.

"May I quote you?"

"Yes, I've always wanted to be a footnote in a scholarly work."

I pretended to read from the book. "In a letter to a friend, Frieseke wrote: I married a natural red-head, as you'll see in the paintings I'm bringing to Owosso…"

Gérard looked surprised. "He really wrote that?"

I burst out laughing. "Not exactly."

"I can't wait to read your article. *ARTnews* is going to have a big bump in sales."

I resumed reading: "In fact, Frieseke did say: 'I am more free in France. There are not the Puritanical restrictions which prevail in America – here I can paint the nude out of doors.'"

"The scourge of America, those Puritans."

"It says here on Frieseke's first visit back home to Owosso in 1902, he told a friend, 'I get much pleasure in shocking the good Church people with the nudes.'"

Gérard chuckled. "Such a rogue. I tell you Giverny was crawling with these blokes. A den of hedonism it was. Imagine it – right here, naked nymphs frolicking in the ferns." He sat up. "Let me see that book again."

Together we looked at the thumbnail photos of the *Le Vivier* nudes.

"They're quite lovely, actually" Gérard said. "Very Renoir-esque. I like this one…" He pointed to a Lawton Parker painting called *The Bather*. The naked model stood on one foot, leaning over, with one leg bent, as if removing a stocking. Her long uncombed golden hair hung freely around her shoulders. Her breasts were in shadow but her thigh caught the light. Gérard's finger traced the curve of her hip. "Nice," he said.

I looked up at the shelter of branches above us, trying to imagine those languorous summer days here.

The green leaves of the past summer were gone. Flecks of red and orange clung to the branches, a few leaves drifting to the surface of the pond, as if a curtain were slowly falling. I took it all in, wanting to memorize the moment.

I felt drawn to this place, to Giverny. I couldn't explain it. It was more than the paintings and the scenes that had inspired them. It was Giverny's stories that stirred me. Its delightful cast of characters, carefree spirit and playful naughtiness.

But something else was stirring inside me as well. My feelings for Gérard. Our faces were a breath apart as we sat looking at the book. I could smell his aftershave. I wondered what it would be like to kiss him.

He turned his head toward me. We looked at each other for a moment. There was no awkwardness. He leaned closer and his mouth was on mine.

His kiss was tender. "Kate," he whispered. He pulled back a little. "Are you okay with this?"

"I think so." I smiled at him.

"Good."

There were no more words during what happened next. There *are* no words for what happens under the intoxicating spell of desire.

~

We lingered at *Le Vivier* for a while. Our clothes stayed on. It was a nippy September day – not ideal for throwing undies to the wind. But we freely let caution take wing.

This was as close to having sex as I'd had in months. My occasional boyfriend in L.A. was more of a buddy with benefits. It hadn't started that way. But neither of us was interested in a full-on commitment. So my love life – and the rest of me – came in spurts.

I had no idea if Gérard had been with other women since the debacle with his fiancée. Nicole had mentioned

Julie, the decorator, and her visits to Giverny that had gotten the local hens clucking.

But if I had to guess, given his sexual energy that afternoon, Gérard had been sorely missing the feel and touch of a woman.

As we were leaving, he locked the gate, then turned to me. I brushed some dead grass from his jacket.

"Well, that was quite the outing," he said.

"You give great tours."

"Kate, I…"

"What?" I was so afraid he might apologize.

"Are you okay?" he asked, again.

"Very."

"Me, too." He smiled and held my hand as we walked back to the moulin.

～

Gérard had an appointment in Vernon that afternoon. I had a pile of tourist-bureau booklets to read, but I couldn't concentrate.

I walked along the Ru for a bit, then sat at the spot where Robinson had set up his easel when he painted Père Trognon fording the stream on his horse. I had a postcard of that painting in my jacket pocket. I studied it for a minute. The stonework of the bridge and even the bend of the iron railing were exactly the same.

During his last summer in Giverny, in 1892, Robinson painted *La Débâcle*, which would be his last painting of Marie. I could envision her sitting on the stone ledge at the far side of the bridge, her shoulder resting on the railing, one hand hooked around its base. With her other hand, she held a little yellow book on her lap, as she gazed across the stream seemingly lost in thought.

What would they have talked about as she posed for him? The latest gossip in the village? *Was it true Radimský was having an affair with one of his models?* And then he'd smile, as if to say, *Who are we to talk?* The slight brim of her stylish hat didn't offer much shade. *Would you like to take a break,* he'd ask. She'd arch her back and gently roll her head, loosening the knots that come when sitting still for so long.

He'd take her upstairs to his studio at the moulin. She'd remove her hat and slip out of her lovely summery dress. He'd loosen her corset. She'd inhale, letting her lungs fill, and then sigh. He'd remove the combs holding back her hair, running his fingers through her chestnut tresses. *This* was the picture he wanted to paint – of the woman he loved, standing before him in the moments before she would give herself to him. The gossips who washed their clothes by the bridge would know the secret of their afternoon trysts, and perhaps there were other secrets, too. But none of it mattered to Theo and Marie. Life was meant to be lived in the moment. And on that summer afternoon, their lovemaking was all that mattered. Like the water cascading over the wheel below them, waves of passion washed over them. On that day, they didn't know of the profound sadness that was to come, the bitter tears they would drown in. On that sweet day, they knew only deep, abiding love. That truly was all that mattered.

~

Nicole had invited Gérard and me to a party at the lodge that evening. On the last day of each painting session, she turned the studio space into a salon where her students could exhibit their work.

As Gérard and I walked through the front gate, I was surprised to see the crowd that had gathered in the garden. Nicole had gracefully insinuated herself into the social scene of Giverny. She knew the local merchants and dignitaries, the curators at the museum, the staff at the Baudy, and the gossiping grannies who were her inside track on what was happening in the village. All groups were represented that night. This would be her final party of the season. Even the mayor of Giverny was there.

Nicole waved from across the patio and came to greet us. *"Bienvenue, chéris!"* She kissed us both. Her eyes held mine for an instant. I wondered if she sensed the pheromones I was excreting from every pore.

I was pretty sure I wouldn't be sleeping alone at the moulin that night. When Gérard had returned from Vernon that afternoon, he had found me on the patio reading. He had brought me a glass of wine and sat down on the chaise next to me.

"So you're leaving tomorrow?" I could hear the sadness in his voice.

I nodded. I had to get back to Paris to file my article. In those days, in 2004, Giverny wasn't exactly a wi-fi hotspot.

"Paris isn't far away," I said, hoping he wanted this to continue. "You promised me French-Mex, remember?"

He smiled. "I'm a man of my word."

In a way, I wasn't really at Nicole's party that night. It was all a blur. I tried to focus on the artwork and the people I was meeting. But all I could think about was what had happened that afternoon at *Le Vivier*. Gérard and I stayed with each other at the party. He knew all the locals, of course, and graciously introduced me. One of the grannies sized me up. I stifled a giggle when I later saw her stealing a glance at me as she chatted with one of her cronies.

Nicole's French chef had produced an amazing buffet. I was ravenously hungry, suddenly feeling my calorie-burn from earlier in the day.

Gérard noticed my loaded plate. "I like a woman with an appetite," he teased.

"How else do you expect me to keep the fire burning?"

He leaned close and whispered, "I'm ready to leave anytime you are."

I looked longingly at my plate.

"After your carb-load, *chérie*," He laughed. "Let me get you some more wine to go with that."

As Gérard walked away, Nicole's voice was suddenly in my ear. "*So?*"

I spun around. "Hello. The new Madame Baudy of Giverny. Great party."

She looked at me intently for a moment and then said, "You've had sex."

I choked on a canapé. "Must be those oysters I just ate." A lame attempt at deflection.

"You and Gérard? I don't believe it."

"What don't you believe?"

"You and Gérard!"

Her incredulity baffled me. It was as if I had betrayed her. For an instant, I wondered if she was lusting after Gérard.

There was no time for discussion. Gérard was returning with the wine.

"Wonderful party, Nicole," he said.

"So happy you're both enjoying yourselves," she said gaily. "If you'll excuse me just one minute – I need to check on something in the kitchen. We have a big surprise for dessert."

I watched Nicole flit away and wondered when I'd have to answer for my non-confession. But at that moment, I didn't care. Nothing else mattered but the man who was offering me a glass of Bordeaux.

~

Gérard followed me up the stairs of the moulin. No sweet parting at the front door as we had done the night before. I held onto the banister, wanting to steady myself. I knew in a matter of moments…

Incredibly, we didn't go crazy. Gérard took the lead. This would be a slow dance, which aroused me even more. God, I wanted him. By the time he had slowly undressed me, I *ached* for him.

I lay like a nude Frieseke model on the fairy-tale bed, watching him undress in the soft candlelight. He didn't take his burning eyes off me as he peeled away his clothes, revealing a gorgeous body toned by all his physical labor. This was a new form of foreplay for me. I was throbbing inside by the time he stood naked next to the bed. But this wasn't a man about to pounce. I saw in him vulnerability, an open wound. He was coming to my bed from a place of great pain.

It was the tenderness of our first night together that stays with me still. The first of many, many nights that he would bring me to new realms of ecstasy. But the nights at the moulin were extraordinary. In my moments of orgasm, I would see a flash image of two lovers from long ago, hearing their moans of pleasure and words of love in the rushing water of the Ru.

5

My return to Paris was a jolt. I had lingered at the moulin the next day, after my night with Gérard. We had great trouble saying good-bye.

Giverny is about an hour from Paris, by train or car. I wasn't going to the edge of the earth. We made plans to see each other soon.

But when the taxi let me out in front of my building on Rue Bonaparte, I felt like I had been shot out of a canon.

It was already dark by the time I got back. The entrance to my building sat at the back of a courtyard, accessed by an 18th-century carriage tunnel. A charming feature, except that the light switch to the tunnel was 10 feet beyond the security door at the street. At night, the tunnel was pitch black. As I groped my way along the wall, feeling for the switch, I felt like I was in a time warp, searching for a way back to my 21st-century life in Paris.

Gérard and I spoke by phone every day. He had begun replacing the gatehouse roof in earnest. The weather was closing in. I had a busy first week back tying up loose ends with my Giverny article, and then I got a plum assignment from a travel magazine that took me to Venice for a week.

There was always something that spoiled our plans to meet. I began to wonder if our little romance had just been an aberration, borne of Giverny's magic.

One day in November, he called to say he was coming to Paris to tend to some business. He was arriving the next morning. Would I meet him at his hotel for dinner?

There were snow flurries in the air as I walked across the Pont Royal the following night. I caught a few of them on my tongue. It was the first snowfall of winter. The first snow I had seen in years.

Gérard was waiting in the lobby of the hotel when I arrived. I didn't see him at first. I took off the wool scarf I had wrapped around my head, shaking snowflakes from my hair. I turned to see him standing by the bar, grinning. Instantly I knew all was well.

He folded me in his arms, squeezing the chill from my bones. "How I've missed you," he whispered.

He had reserved a table at the hotel restaurant, which boasted a Michelin star. He was wining and dining me. I could feel myself glowing.

We slipped back easily to where we had been. There was so much to talk about. I showed him my photos of Venice. He showed me pictures of the new gatehouse roof. He had begun the interior work. But all that could wait, he said.

He reached over and took my hand. "I don't want to wait this long again."

"Me either."

He told me he was going to an auction the next day. Julie, his designer, had some pieces she wanted him to see. I felt a twinge of unease at the mention of her name. I remembered Nicole telling me about her frequent visits to the moulin and the granny gossip. I hadn't actually seen Nicole since my Giverny visit. She had been traveling to art shows. We, too, kept trying to make a date to meet. I didn't make a huge effort, though, fearing an interrogation about what had happened with Gérard. But I knew she was back working at the gallery in my neighborhood. I wouldn't be able to postpone the inquisition for too long.

We had just been served dessert and coffee when Gérard suddenly looked distracted. I turned to see a slim, attractive woman coming in from the lobby.

"Gérard, there you are!" She hurried toward our table.

He looked stunned. "What are you doing here?"

For a split second, I imagined the worst. His ex-fiancée had come looking for him. *Except this woman was French, not English.* He had found a new girlfriend since I last saw him. *No, he wouldn't be with me tonight if he had.* In a moment like that, it's interesting to realize what unshakeable truths you hold about someone.

"I couldn't wait until tomorrow," the woman said excitedly. She looked at me apologetically. "I'm so sorry to intrude."

She wasn't at all sorry. This was a gorgeous raven-haired Alpha female marking her turf.

She extended her hand to me. *"Je suis Julie."*

As Julie took my hand, I feared her long red nails might extract blood. I didn't bother telling her my name. I had a feeling she already knew it.

I could see anger rising in Gérard, a side of him I hadn't seen. I suddenly felt like the three of us were in a bad French movie. They were speaking rapid French. I needed subtitles. Actually, I needed to pee.

"If you'll excuse me…" I pushed back my chair. As I stood up, I got a good whiff of Julie's perfume – Eau de Bourbon or was it Jacques Daniels?

"Kate!" Gérard was on his feet before I was.

"I'm going to the ladies room. I'll be back." But I really wanted to get my coat and go.

I took my time. I stood in front of the elegant mirror in the anteroom of the ladies' salon, taking a good look at myself. The glow from earlier in the evening was gone. In fact, I looked like I had just been run over by a horse carriage. I suddenly felt very tired.

When I returned to the table, Gérard was on his phone. Julie was gone. He stood up and pulled out my chair. He was still speaking French. But I got the gist this time. He kept saying *no, Julie, no.*

He abruptly ended the call and sat down. He looked devastated. "Kate, I'm so sorry about this."

"Should I be upset?"

"It spoiled what I had hoped would be a lovely evening."

I nodded, but I didn't have the energy to talk about it. "It was a lovely evening," I assured him.

But in that moment, I closed the door to spending the night together. The fatal moment when the present slips into the past: It *was* a lovely evening. I could see his disappointment. But I wasn't going to spend the night with him, not with Madame Alpha lurking.

We'd both lost our appetite for dessert. The maître d' presented my coat. The bellman flagged a taxi. I kissed Gérard on the cheek and politely thanked him for dinner. He walked me to the curb and opened the taxi door for me, taking over the bellman's job.

"I'll call you tomorrow," he said. "I'm truly sorry, Kate."

I squeezed his arm as I got into the taxi. I said nothing because I didn't know what to say.

~

The next morning when I woke up, it only took a few seconds before the day turned gray. In those precious first seconds of a new day, the weather instantly can turn dark with a bad memory from the night before.

Fighting the urge to pull the covers over my head, I firmly planted my feet on the floor. My fuzzy pink bunny slippers were always a comfort to me on bleak mornings.

It was past 10 when I arrived at the *boulangerie*. I knew I had already missed Nicole. I couldn't face her that morning. I didn't want to see anyone that morning.

But that wasn't to be. I had just stepped into the shop and inhaled the heavenly scent of French roast when I saw him sitting at a table in the corner. Gérard was waiting for me.

My heart did a little handstand. But I played it cool. He joined me at the counter.

"Are you stalking me?" I asked.

"Yes." He smiled. "Nicole told me I might see you here."

Oh great, I thought. *Now Nicole is in the mix.*

"What would you like?" he asked as I eyed the pastry case.

"Something obscenely sweet." I needed comfort food.

"What about this?" He pointed to the French version of a Bear Claw.

I nodded. He bought two. We returned to his corner table with our treats and coffee.

In a strategic maneuver, I quickly sank my teeth into the gooey pastry. I didn't want to start the conversation, which I wouldn't be able to do with my mouth full. I chewed slowly, waiting for him to begin.

"Is it as good as Henri's?" he asked.

I shook my head *no*.

He took a bite. "Not bad. But not Henri." He sipped his coffee as I continued chewing slowly. "Kate…about last night."

"I think that's a movie title," I said with my mouth full. (So much for strategy.) The bad French film appeared to be continuing.

"What's that American expression – can you give me some slack?"

"Can you *cut* me some slack."

"Can you?" He looked a little ragged around the edges.

"How long have you been sitting here?"

He glanced at his watch. "Two hours. And I hardly slept last night."

I looked at him sympathetically. "Talk to me."

He sighed. "Julie is a friend…"

And so began the story: He met Julie during their university days in Paris. She married his roommate Philippe, who also became an architect. Gérard was the best man at their wedding. They visited him often in London. They went skiing together in Gstaad every winter. They were his *best* friends.

"When I became engaged to Pamela, they spent New Year's with us in London. We had a fantastic time. A month later, we all went to Gstaad together. Pamela wasn't much of a skier. But she seemed happy to be there."

I could see the strain in his face. Then he said, "She and Philippe really hit it off."

"How do you mean?"

"They started an affair that continued back in London. Philippe was there a lot working on a project…"

"*What?*"

"I found out three months before the wedding. My best friend was fucking my fiancée."

He looked at me with such sadness. My heart ached for him.

"Julie is still furious and wants to get even with him. He's still seeing Pamela. But Julie won't divorce him – don't ask me why. I think she secretly wants him back. It's totally fucked up."

"Wow."

"Julie's been a big help with the work at the moulin. She's a fabulous decorator with lots of connections and great ideas. We've spent a lot of time together. She's a good friend. But I don't want more than that. I know she's unhappy and lonely. And so am I…"

"Why did she come to the hotel last night?"

"She'd had a little to drink, as you may have noticed."

I nodded.

"She knew I was seeing you for dinner."

"You told her about me?"

"Just that I had met you in Giverny and had asked you for dinner. But apparently, she'd heard more than that from Nicole. They've recently become friends, it seems."

"Ahhh...the plot thickens." I smiled at him. "Just so you know, I haven't discussed you with Nicole."

"I don't care about that. I care about *you*..." He reached across the table and took my hand. "And your very sticky fingers."

We both laughed. A much-needed moment of comic relief, provided by French Bear-Claw honey glaze.

"So what happened to Julie last night?"

"I put her in a taxi and sent her home."

"That was two women you sent home in cabs last night."

"The hotel barman enjoyed the show. He gave me a nightcap that was supposed to put me to sleep."

"Which didn't work."

"It was on the house." He shrugged. "You get what you pay for."

"What time is the auction today?"

He shook his head. "I'm not going. I'm totally knackered."

"Hmmm." I stroked his hand with my sticky fingers. "I know a little place near here where you could take a nap."

He smiled. "Sounds wonderful."

~

Gérard loved the carriage tunnel and started telling me about the architectural history of the neighborhood. But his enthusiasm waned when we hit the fourth flight of stairs.

"You didn't mention this little place was a hundred steps above street level." He looked up at the next flight and moaned.

"Only 77. C'mon. We're almost there."

We fell into my little bed, happy lovers. We spent the entire day in that bed. Our lovemaking quickly healed the wound of the night before. In the way he held me, I knew I was in the arms of a man who, if I let him, would love, protect and cherish me. I suppose it was a bit soon to have those thoughts. But sometimes you just *know*.

We took a long nap that afternoon, tucked snugly under a fluffy duvet, as winter shadows crept across the room. I couldn't remember when I had ever felt so content.

That night was sheer bliss...we ate Mexican. And the guacamole was amazingly good.

6

Gérard spent a week with me in Paris. He checked out of the hotel and stayed at my place. We were good flat mates, even in cozy quarters. He loved my apartment, with its view of mansard rooftops and the cobbled courtyard below. We made simple meals in my tiny corner kitchen and kept a tray of snacks and a bottle of wine by the bed. We spent a lot of time in bed.

I was besotted with Gérard. With any other man, I would have been hearing alarm sirens warning me not to fall hard. I hadn't been lucky in love. My romances were usually short-lived. Or they drifted into nothingness.

But with Gérard, I wanted to leap into a free fall. I knew he'd catch me, caress me, coddle me. Our sex was spectacular. I felt totally uninhibited, giving myself to him with abandon. I was *alive* in a way I had never known before.

We ventured out into the real world occasionally. We took walks along the Seine, looking like lovers you see on Paris postcards. We did a sweet re-enactment of Robert Doisneau's famous photo of the couple kissing in the grand square by the Hôtel de Ville. We asked an American guy – who was visiting Paris with his new bride, as it turned out – to take the shot. He framed it perfectly, with the architectural elements (so loved by Gérard) behind us and me leaning back, Gérard's arm firmly around my shoulder as he planted that Big Kiss.

Gérard and I worked a little culture into our wanderings. We spent a lovely afternoon on the trail of Monet. Gérard took me to a museum on the edge of Paris I hadn't visited before – Musée Marmottan Monet, which contains the world's largest collection of Monet paintings, bequeathed to the museum by his son Michel. The centerpiece of the collection is Monet's painting *Impression, soleil levant* (*Impression, Sunrise*), stolen from the museum by armed thieves in broad daylight in 1985 and recovered five years later. It's the painting that gave a name to the Impressionist movement – a term coined by an art critic intending to discredit the innovative painting style of this radical group led by Monet. In 1874, 30 artists including Monet, Renoir, Cézanne, Degas, Sisley, Morisot and Pissarro held an exhibition of their work in Paris that rocked the art establishment of the day. It was the dawn of modern art.

We wandered into a small room where caricature portraits were on display. At first, I couldn't believe they were the work of Monet. As a teenager growing up in the Normandy port town of Le Havre, he earned pocket money by doing caricatures of townspeople, which he sold at a local frame shop. The shop owner showed the sketches to French artist Eugène Boudin, who took the boy under wing. Boudin showed him how to use oils and pastels and paint landscapes *en plein air*. To think that Monet could have ended up as a cartoonist if he hadn't had the good fortune of finding a mentor who steered him toward the path he was meant to take. Apparently, Monet wasn't totally convinced he had chosen the right path, however. He's often quoted as saying that if he had continued working as a cartoonist, "I'd be a millionaire today."

Gérard and I ended up that day at the Musée de l'Orangerie where Monet's water lily panels were installed a year after his death. Monet donated the murals to the French nation, shattered by the First World War, intending the museum to be a refuge for meditation and a monument to peace.

At the Orangerie's two water-lily galleries, Gérard and I sat on the long benches, taking in the nuances of Monet's masterwork. I wished I had visited the gardens with Gérard while I was in Giverny.

"I want to see the lily pond in spring, with the wisteria blooming on the bridge," I told him.

He squeezed my hand. "We will go."

The week ended too quickly, of course, and our schedules weren't allowing any wiggle room. I was leaving in a few days for Chicago, for the opening of the Impressionist exhibition. Gérard was expecting deliveries at the moulin the following week for the next phase of the gatehouse renovation.

He was looking at my wall calendar on our last day together. "When will you be back?"

"December 2nd."

"Two weeks," he said.

I'd be spending Thanksgiving with college friends from Northwestern. We had been planning this reunion for months. I knew they'd love Gérard.

I slipped my arms around his waist. "Any chance you could get away?"

He smiled at me. "I'll try."

～

Winter that year in Chicago arrived early with a vengeance. I was reminded of my student days, when I rode the L train from Evanston into the city for an art-appreciation class that was offered at the Art Institute. One January morning, it was so cold on the platform, I thought my eyeballs had frozen. When I got off the train that day, I ran into the nearest office building and found a restroom in the lobby. In one of my soulful bathroom-mirror conversations with myself, I vowed I'd go back to southern California after graduation. I wasn't equipped to survive in the sub-arctic tundra of Chicago.

But there I was, 20 years later, bundled up like a baby, back on an L platform. It was 20 degrees and windy. The heat lamp above me glowed orange, but my toes, inside of my leather boots, were numb.

I had a short walk to the Art Institute and hurried up the front steps. I stood in the museum's grand foyer, luxuriating in the comforting blast of heat and the wonderful feeling of being back in a place I loved. I had spent many hours at the Art Institute during my college years. I loved that art-history class, which primarily focused on the museum's vast collection. I'd arrive early and sometimes linger at the museum until closing. I hoped I'd have some time to wander around later that day. I had many old friends there – painted by Monet, Van Gogh, Renoir, Degas, Cézanne, Cassatt and Seurat – that I wanted to see.

The American Impressionist show was opening to the public in a few days. My editor at *ARTnews* had arranged for me to attend a preview tour led by the exhibition's curator, Sonia Hillard. He had liked the Giverny piece I had written, and with my art-history background, wanted to use me for future assignments. He had even mentioned the possibility of me becoming a regular contributor.

I picked up a pass that was waiting for me at the museum membership office. The tour would start in an hour, but the woman at the desk told me the exhibition's galleries were open to pass-holders if I'd like to take a look.

A guard at the exhibit entrance handed me a brochure. Several other early birds had arrived ahead of me. In a few days, these rooms would be packed with visitors. I felt so lucky to have this chance, to see these works in solitude.

I stepped into the first gallery and was instantly blown away. The exhibit included several paintings from the museum in Giverny, alongside many others that had been culled from museums and collections around the world.

There were stunning paintings by Frieseke I had never seen, of his Giverny garden scenes with elegantly dressed women surrounded by sun-speckled flowerbeds.

The nude by Lawton Parker that Gérard had admired was on display. It took me back to that day at *Le Vivier*. I closed my eyes for a moment, willing Gérard to appear next to me. Sadly, I needed to work on my teleporting powers.

I was drawn to a painting of a little girl with short blonde hair standing by a wooden gate. She held a clump of cherries, looking a bit anxious as if she had been caught red-handed – and indeed she had, literally and otherwise. The painting was aptly titled *A Marauder*. I leaned over to look at the tag on the wall, to read the artist's name.

Theodore Robinson.

I stood transfixed. I had never seen this painting, not even in a book. The painting wasn't mentioned in the brochure the guard had given me. Hopefully, I'd find it in the exhibition catalog.

In the next gallery, Robinson was in his glory. I saw Père Trognon fording the stream by the moulin. On the opposite wall, the Butler wedding party marched from Giverny's *mairie*. There was a lovely painting of Marie sitting on the hillside above Giverny that I had seen in one of my books. Robinson paid close attention to her facial features – the delicate curve of her nose, her full upper lip. There was no doubt in my mind they had been lovers. I knew he had kissed those sensuous lips many times.

And then there was Robinson's *pièce de résistance*: *La Débâcle*. The painting was far more compelling in real life than on the page. I could almost feel the texture of the paint, the way the delicate blue and pink stripes of Marie's dress traced the outline of her figure. I knew the coolness and roughness of the railing that she held. I had held that railing, too.

I could hear the muffled chatter between Theodore and Marie as she posed. She tried not to laugh at something he had said. She needed to hold her gaze as his brush traced on his canvas the outline of her eyebrows and cheekbones – everything about her that he knew in intimate detail.

He would take her to his studio at the moulin on that hot summer's afternoon. She'd drink from a ladle that sat in a bucket of cool water and let the water run down her chin, her neck. He'd trace the rivulet with his finger, between her breasts…

I took a deep breath – *god, I missed Gérard.* I quickly needed to re-focus.

I returned to the little girl with the cherries. Robinson had captured her genuine remorse. She seemed to be handing him the cherries as a gift, asking for forgiveness, but not before she had tasted the sweetness of her plunder. She had a Dutch Boy haircut and was wearing a soiled pale blue dress. I impulsively wanted to hug her.

I stood there for several minutes, creating a story about her. And then I heard a man's voice behind me.

"You're here," he said softly, as if he didn't believe it was really me.

I turned around, wondering who had just appeared from my past. A former teacher from the art program or a college friend?

But to my surprise, there was no one. I was alone in the gallery.

I looked at the little girl again and suddenly felt unsettled. *Who are you?* I whispered to her.

She seemed to be sheepishly handing me the cherries. I wanted to soothe her. She hadn't committed a crime. I imagined taking her in my arms and kissing her, tasting the cherry juice on her plump cheek.

I wandered into a dimly lit adjoining room. I was surprised to see a collection of Robinson's photographs – far more extensive than what I had seen in Giverny. Each photo captured a fleeting moment, an expression, an emotion. A little girl in a big sunhat, pumping water from a cistern. A woman, on a ladder, picking plums. Claude Monet, leaning on a walking stick, looking every inch the peripatetic gardener – in a floppy hat, a baggy jacket and the 1880s version of 501 jeans.

One photo got my attention. Its title was *Girl Lying in Grass*. The young woman, who appears to be in her late teens or early 20s, playfully smiles at the camera. She's not attractive like Marie. She's a local girl, a bit coarse looking. She lies on the grass, elbows in the air, both hands holding the wide brim of her hat. It's a seductive, come-hither pose. Her white peasant blouse, cinched tightly by a belt, reveals the outline of her breasts.

How dare she, I thought.

For some bizarre reason, I felt incensed. I tried to shake it off. I had traversed seven time zones just the day before. I was tired, hungry and every fiber of my heart ached for Gérard. Maybe I just needed a stiff cup of coffee – a nice French roast would do.

I noticed a group was gathering at the exhibit entrance. It was almost time for the tour. I walked past the little marauder with her clump of cherries. I could taste the sweetness on her cheek.

~

Sonia Hillard, the curator, was a delight. An American Impressionist scholar, she had written much of the text for the exhibition catalog – a hefty 200-page book, full of color plates of the paintings, biographies, timelines, and artists' journal writings and correspondence. She had spent six months at the Terra Foundation study center in Giverny doing the research for this show, so she knew the village well and its colorful history.

She led our small group through the exhibition, telling us stories about the life and times of the featured artists. They were familiar characters to me now. I imagined them at the Baudy, having drinks on the terrace or painting under the shade trees in Angélina's garden. When Sonia spoke of *Le Hameau*, I could smell the lilies and hear the clatter of teacups.

Sonia was a big Robinson fan, which was not only evident by the wall space she had given to his work, but by her enthusiasm as she talked about his technique, his relationship with Monet and his personality that had come to life for her during her research. Robinson had kept detailed journals and was a prolific letter writer. There was a section in the exhibition book devoted to his correspondence with Monet. I smiled to myself, thinking of Madame Mallery calling Robinson a *minor* artist.

In a gallery I hadn't seen before the tour started, Sonia showed us Robinson's painting of Marie in a walled garden, called *The Layette*, inspired by the photo I had seen at the museum in Giverny. Marie sits on a wooden ladder-back chair, sewing. A child's garment is draped over a bottom rung of the chair.

"This woman is an art-history mystery," Sonia told us. "She was Robinson's favorite model, whom he met in Paris during the spring of 1884, on his second visit to France. She is known only as Marie. We know that she worked as an artist's model in Paris – and, in fact, may have posed for Edgar Degas, based on what Robinson wrote about her in his diary, where he refers to her simply as M. She frequently traveled with him to Giverny and was the subject of some gossip. Based on my research, she and Robinson had considered marriage, but decided against it, for reasons that aren't exactly clear. Robinson's poor health might have been an issue."

I wanted to know more about Sonia's research and hoped I could meet with her privately while I was in Chicago.

After the tour, I purchased the exhibition catalog and went to the museum's Reading Room where I had spent many hours as a student. I sat at one of the long oak tables under the stained-glass ceiling, surrounded by happy memories of discoveries I had made in that room. *Moments of romantic enchantment*, as Madame Mallery would say.

I quickly scanned the index of the exhibition catalog. As I expected, there was a long list of Robinson references, including several pages devoted to his paintings of Marie. In the book, Sonia writes of their affair and their "reluctant" decision not to marry.

The catalog contained paintings of Marie I had never seen, including Robinson's first depiction of her called *Lady in Red*, from 1885. Her head is turned to her left, showing her striking profile against a leafy background. Her brown hair is pulled back in a twist. Only the shoulders and the scoop neckline of her red dress are visible, with a white undergarment showing slightly where a top button is unfastened.

In a dramatic portrait called *The Red Gown*, Marie stands with her back to the viewer in front of a bower of pink flowers, wearing what appears to be the same red dress. A fold of red fabric falls from the neckline to the ground in this immense painting that's slightly more than six feet in height. Marie rests her left hand on an arched branch, in a graceful, romanticized pose. Her head is turned to the left. In all of his paintings of Marie, except for one, Robinson shows Marie in profile. The exception, called *Reverie*, depicts her sitting on a wooden chair and holding a violin. Again, she wears the red dress – presumably a studio prop – along with a white cap that conceals most of her hair. She looks directly at the viewer – at Robinson – but her somber gaze reveals little about her.

Apparently, Marie was an accomplished pianist. In the spring of 1887, Robinson painted her in *At the Piano*, at the Paris residence of wealthy art patron John Armstrong "Archie" Chanler, a descendant of John Jacob Astor. She wears a white dress and pearl-drop earrings, as she plays from sheet music at a grand piano. The cream-paneled salon gives the painting a luminous feel. A pot of white flowers sits by a leg of the piano, balancing the composition with a feminine flourish.

The same year, Marie posed for Robinson at an upright piano, which bears a close resemblance to the piano in the dining room of the Baudy. Robinson's first extended stay in Giverny happened that summer. It seems Marie was his traveling companion or at least spent some time with him there during that visit.

The exhibition catalog contained a photo of Robinson – the first photo I had ever seen of him. He's seated at an easel, in a wooded setting, with a young man behind him – a fellow American artist named Kenyon Cox, who's leaning against a tree and smoking a cigarette. They're both looking at Robinson's painting on the easel, which isn't visible to the camera. Robinson's face is partially obscured by a large beret that's pulled down over his eyes. He has a droopy moustache and is wearing a voluminous smock. At the neckline, you can see a shirt collar and a scarf tied in a bow. Cox looks like he belongs on the cover of a men's fashion magazine – he has the suave look of a bohemian painter, his open jacket revealing a long watch chain. The upturned brim up his hat is at a jaunty angle. But Robinson is every inch the artist-at-work.

I could feel myself hitting the wall of jet lag, so I packed up and headed back to the hotel. There was a phone message from Gérard. It was nearly midnight his time. But I knew he'd want to hear from me, so I called him when I got to the room.

"*Chérie*, it's you." He sounded sleepy. "I was hoping you'd call tonight."

At a dollar a minute, we didn't talk long. He was glad to hear I'd had a good first day and told me his big news: He had booked a flight to Chicago and would be arriving in five days. Though it seemed like an eternity, I was over the moon.

"Gérard, I miss you so much."

"I miss you, too, my love."

My love. The sound of that felt wonderful.

~

I spent the next few days doing more research about Robinson. My editor at *ARTnews* was interested in a follow-up article about the Terra Foundation collection, which gave me an opportunity to meet with Sonia Hillard. She graciously made time in her busy schedule and arranged for us to have lunch at her office.

Unlike Pierre Gaston, Sonia was a burbling fountain of information. She spoke about Robinson as if he were an old friend. She had read his diaries and correspondence.

"He was often described as a generous, kind man – with an infectious laugh and a great sense of humor. Madame Baudy adored him. Have you seen the portrait he painted of her?" Sonia flipped through the exhibition catalog to the portrait, dated 1888. Madame Baudy sits at a small table, wearing a black dress and straw-colored hat. She holds a glass, next to a bottle of wine.

"She looks so young. I had this image of her as this motherly, older woman," I said, looking closely at the portrait.

"She was in her mid-30s when she and her husband opened the hotel in 1887. She died in 1949, in her mid-90s."

"It's incredible to think of the changes she witnessed – and the art history she was a part of."

"More than 350 artists from 18 countries came to Giverny between 1885 and 1915 – can you imagine? The majority were Americans, but artists came from all over Europe, all over the world, in fact – from Australia, Canada, Russia, Argentina. Many of the artists are unknown today. But some are quite famous." Sonia turned to another page in the catalog. "Here's the bill for Paul Cézanne, who stayed at the Baudy for a few weeks in 1894 and rented one of the studios there for his private use."

"When was Robinson's last stay in Giverny?"

"In 1892."

"The year he painted *La Débâcle*."

"Exactly."

"He didn't die until 1896. Why didn't he return to Giverny?"

"He intended to, according to his letters to Monet. But he was in frail health. His financial situation was shaky – and there was an economic crisis in the U.S. at that time. He taught painting classes in Princeton and Philadelphia. He spent time at the Cos Cob Art Colony in Greenwich, Connecticut. He painted in the Catskills and at the New Jersey shore. Early in 1896, he wrote to Monet of his plans to go to Vermont that spring to paint. He told Monet, who was a chef in his own right, about the process of making maple syrup. Robinson described the color of the syrup and the taste. He described the rural scene – the snow in the forests, the sleighs and the oxen. Robinson was born in Vermont and had visited there the summer before. He yearned to return there and work *tranquilly*, he told Monet."

"What happened?"

"A month later, Robinson had a violent asthma attack. It came on suddenly. He died on April 2, in New York City. His close friend Will Low, who had been with him in Giverny, wrote about Robinson's death in his memoir. He said a doctor had seen him that morning…"

Sonia turned to an excerpt, in the catalog, from Low's memoir and read aloud: "…half an hour later, he had expired as a candle, burning brightly down to its socket, flickers and goes out."

We both sat quietly for a moment. My heart ached. Sonia looked at me empathetically. "So sad, isn't it? He had such immense talent. His ascent in the art world was just beginning."

I struggled to find my voice. "What about Marie?"

"Ah, Marie." Sonia smiled. "There's so much we don't know. But it seems she and Theodore had a long love affair. They met soon after he arrived in Paris in 1884. You've seen the early paintings he's done of her?"

I nodded.

"Marie was elegant and refined. An accomplished musician, it seems. She worked as a painter's model in Paris. Robinson tells a story in his diary of her witnessing Paris art dealer Paul Durand-Ruel taking a painting from Degas' studio to make sure he wouldn't do more work on it or scrape it out."

"You said he and Marie had considered marriage."

"Before Robinson's last visit to France – in the spring of 1892 – an artist friend of his came to his studio in New York. The guy had heard that Robinson was going back to France to get married. Robinson wrote in his diary that *the dear boy wanted to talk to me.*" Sonia smiled. "Robinson's diaries are such a joy to read."

"He obviously was with Marie that summer," I said. "He painted her on the bridge."

"It was a summer of weddings that year – Monet married Alice Hoschedé and Theodore Butler married her daughter Suzanne. But there was no wedding for Theodore and Marie. A few years earlier, Robinson had written a letter to Will Low, telling him about Marie and that they had reluctantly decided not to marry."

"But why?"

Sonia shrugged. "He had a chronic illness that hovered over him like a dark cloud. I think he was realistic about his prognosis."

"You mentioned there was gossip about Marie in Giverny. What was that about?"

"How shall I say this?" Sonia looked like she was about to tell me a dark secret about my own mother. "Marie often brought her little *niece* with her to Giverny."

I didn't get what Sonia was suggesting at first. "Why was that a problem?"

"Well, it seems the little girl looked a lot like Robinson."

I was stunned. "There was a love child?"

Sonia got up from her chair and walked over to a bookcase behind her desk. She took a binder off the shelf and came back to the table where we'd been having lunch.

Inside the binder were photocopies of old letters. "This is a collection of correspondence from some of the summer residents at the Baudy," Sonia said. "This particular letter

I'm going to share with you was written by a woman who was staying at the Baudy in 1890."

I wasn't sure I wanted to hear this. Yes, of course, it was part of the mystery that the writer-in-me wanted to solve. But on a deeply personal level, I felt so protective of these two lovers, whose story clearly had been fraught with so much pain.

Sonia read part of the letter: "It looks very strange but Mr. Robinson has a model down here who has her little daughter – I believe she says niece, with her. Everyone says that – well, it seems difficult to say, but that the little girl is the daughter of Mr. Robinson…if true I can easily see why Mr. Robinson's life has been so utterly unhappy – surely an affair to be deplored – the child looks very like him – I've only seen them together once – because while she is here, they all dine with Mme. Baudy…"

And in what felt like a lighting-bolt moment of déjà vu, I saw a little girl with a clump of cherries in her hand – the darling marauder.

7

That night, it snowed. When I opened the curtains of my hotel room the next morning, I suddenly craved butter-milk pancakes with warm maple syrup. I had been living in the land of luscious crêpes. But that morning, I wanted a serious stack of flapjacks.

I was meeting Alex for breakfast at a diner in Evanston we used to go to as students. Alex and I had lived in the same freshman dorm and later moved into a house off-campus with our posse of friends. We were a motley lot back then. We all managed to graduate – some of us with honors, miraculously. But we wept on graduation day, knowing that an amazing chapter of our lives was ending.

We vowed to stay in touch and meet up at least once a year. No excuses allowed for missing the annual reunion. One year, the reunion happened at Alex's wedding. Alex felt he had gotten cheated out of some of the reunion fes-tivities, so he lingered with us at the bar at the reception.

He started doing tequila shots and passed out before he made it to the bridal suite. That didn't endear the group to Carolyn, his new wife, who never forgave us. We tried to redeem ourselves, each in our own way. I sent her a gift certificate to a hotel spa near where she worked in the Loop. She politely thanked me the next time I saw her, but I could tell she needed an untold number of spa treatments to remove the prickles under her skin.

I wasn't shocked when Alex e-mailed me a few weeks before I arrived in Chicago for the exhibition, saying that he and Carolyn had separated. They were in counseling, but he didn't sound hopeful that the marriage could be saved. I knew the group consensus would affirm his doubts. I had correctly assumed our Thanksgiving celebration would not include Carolyn.

A gust of icy wind blew me in through the front door of the diner. Alex was quickly on his feet. I could tell he desperately needed a hug. I immediately noticed he had aged a bit. The old laugh lines were deeper and he was grayer at the temples. But he was as darling as ever.

"God, you look great, my scrumptious crêpe suzette," he said as he embraced me.

"You do, too." I'd had a big crush on Alex when we were freshmen. He still had a way of taking my breath away with his *joie de vivre* and his big bear hugs.

He had snagged the corner table where we all used to hang out, under the autographed photos of distinguished Northwestern alums like Ann-Margret, Charlton Heston, Cindy Crawford and David Schwimmer. Alex once had slipped an autographed photo of himself into David

Schwimmer's frame. It stayed there for weeks before the diner owner noticed. He gave Alex his own frame and hung his photo over the men's room door.

As if reading my mind, Alex pointed toward the men's room. "Check it out – I'm still on the wall of shame."

"You deserve more respect, Dr. Alex. Congratulations, by the way. Are you on the *New York Times* bestseller list yet?"

"Actually..."

"Seriously? When did this happen?"

He smiled. "I got a call from my agent yesterday."

"My god, Alex. That's wonderful!" I reached across the table and squeezed his arm. "We need to celebrate."

He patted my hand. "We will."

Alex had gotten a doctorate in psychology and written a book, based on his thesis, about the effective use of humor in psychotherapy, which catapulted him into the talk-show circuit. He was a frequent guest on a radio show in Chicago. With his engaging on-air personality, he had a big following of loyal listeners.

His new book was on regression therapy – the exploration of forgotten or repressed experiences from the past that can affect physical, emotional and mental health.

"I helped get you on the bestseller list. I bought a copy at the airport."

"For that, my dear, I'll buy you breakfast. The usual?"

I nodded, as the waitress appeared.

"She'll have the Wildcat Special, tall stack," he said, smiling at me. "Forget that little Dixie cup of maple syrup. She wants the jug."

～

For the next hour, Alex and I shared the intimate details of our lives. I told him about Gérard and he told me about the demise of his marriage.

"Things got really bad about six months ago." Alex looked out the window for a moment, staring at nothing in particular. "Carolyn had a miscarriage."

"Oh, Alex. I'm so sorry."

"It really threw her into a spin." He gave the saltshaker a twirl. "She blames me."

"*You?*"

"She says I didn't want the baby and I poisoned her with my *toxicity*. That's the word she uses. Toxicity."

"Did you want the baby?" I could see the pain in his eyes. "Sorry. You don't have to answer that. "

"No, don't apologize. That's a question I need to answer. And you're probably the only person I could say this to…" He looked at me with such sadness. "No. I didn't want to raise a child with Carolyn. Maybe she's right…"

"Alex, don't do this to yourself."

"I know, I know. But I feel tremendous guilt."

"You didn't cause the miscarriage. She lost the baby because there was something wrong with the fetus. Or with her. Or maybe the baby didn't want her as a mother. I don't know why these things happen. But I think, as sad as it is, that little soul is in a better place."

Alex looked at me for a moment. His jaw muscles were tense. I knew he was struggling to hold himself together. And then he said softly, "God, Kate, I love you."

I knew his words came from that place where old friends reside. Where love is unconditional and helps heal the deepest wounds.

～

Alex wanted to know about my life in Paris and my work. I told him about the assignment that had taken me to Giverny.

"Something strange happened to me at the moulin. I haven't even told this to Gérard…"

Alex held up his hand, with his little finger extended. I locked my little finger around his. A Pinkie Promise was a solemn oath never to reveal what was about to be spoken – even under the influence of tequila shots. Our group had made many Pinkie Promises over the years.

As I told him the story of my first night all alone at the moulin, Alex looked at me wide-eyed. "Jeez, Kate. You should be writing horror stories."

"It was a little creepy at first. But then I sang to him…"

"The phantom?"

"You think I've lost it, don't you?"

"It *is* my profession to assess degrees of craziness. On a scale of one to 10 – 10 being stark-raving mad – I'd say you're somewhere around a five."

"Really?"

"Maybe a six."

"Stop!"

Alex laughed. "Okay, four-and-a-half. Tops."

"Don't laugh, please."

"Okay." He tried to look serious.

"That first night I sang to him, I felt so calm. I slept so well that night. I actually felt comforted by his presence."

"How many nights were you alone with *him*?"

"One-two-three…" I counted on my fingers. "Three nights, but not the last."

Alex raised an eyebrow.

"Gérard."

"Of course. *And?* If I may be so rude."

"Amazing." I sighed.

"What's with these French guys?"

"*Je ne sais quoi.*"

Alex playfully rolled his eyes.

"But that's not the end of my phantom story."

I told Alex about Marie and what happened at the exhibition preview, as I stood at the painting of the little marauder. "Alex, the voice was so clear. *You're here*, he said. I turned around fully expecting to see someone behind me. But there was no one there."

"Okay, sweetie, you're up to an eight."

"Alex!"

He smiled at me. "Kate, there's a lot to talk about here. We can't cover it all over a stack of pancakes." He looked at my near-empty plate. "You've done a good job there, by the way. Do you have enough syrup?"

I laughed. "Yes, I'm good."

"The 10-cent version of my $25 book is that you may be experiencing what some would call a past-life encounter."

"What would you call it?"

"I don't have a label to stick on this." He gave the salt-shaker another spin. "The sub-conscious mind is a complicated animal. But there is a substantial body of research that has explored a deep spiritual connection to forgotten or repressed past experiences. The purpose of regression therapy is to help people discover and relive earlier experiences that might be causing present emotional or physical problems. If there's something unresolved from your past, it may be affecting you now."

"What about from a past life?"

"Reincarnation is the core tenant of many religions and tribal societies. Who am I to debunk that? I interviewed a guy for the book who told me a fascinating story about being reincarnated as his mother's fiancée, who died in World War II. It had taken him awhile to come to this realization. But he was totally okay with it. In fact, he saw it as a gift – a way to keep this man's memory alive for his mother."

"How wonderful that he could see it that way."

"He said some things that really stuck with me. He was talking about what he called *cellular memory*. He said everything we experience in life registers in the cells of our bodies. This includes all of the experiences we've had in all of our lifetimes. When our cumulative soul, as he called it, takes on form and enters a physical body, all of these memories come along with it and quietly reside in the cells of the body. Which explains why certain sights, sounds or smells can suddenly trigger thoughts or visions or impressions from other lifetimes."

"Déjà vu."

"Exactly." Alex smiled at me. "He said at the soul level – on that level of consciousness deep inside our hearts – we know who we once were and what choices and decisions we need to make and directions we need to take in our current lifetime. Our souls give us subtle hints to guide us. A beautiful definition of intuition, isn't it?"

I nodded. "Maybe I'm not so crazy?"

Alex reached over and took my hand. "Sweetie, you're not crazy. You're an amazing woman, so strong and brave. My god, I couldn't have spent a night alone in an old mill with a phantom on the loose." He grinned at me. "You have an inspiring sense of adventure and a willingness to open every pore of your heart and soul to the new worlds you're discovering. Don't shut yourself off to any of it. Live it. You're a writer – write about it."

Suddenly, I couldn't stop the tears.

Alex held my hand tighter. "I don't know what this story means. The artist, his lover, the little girl. Who knows – maybe you were that wench lying in the grass."

Alex is the only person I know who can make me laugh and cry at the same time.

"I can see you standing under the vault in that room at the mill, singing to your phantom. In perfect pitch, in perfect resonance. Trust that there's a life lesson – or maybe a gift from the universe – in this."

"Thank you, Alex." I dabbed my tears with my napkin. "Maybe Gérard is the gift?"

"You've really fallen for this guy, haven't you?"

"I have. I've waited so long for him, Alex."

He kissed my hand. "I know, sweetie. I know."

8

Two days later, Gérard arrived in Chicago. His flight was an hour late. The weather was bad that night. I stuck to the plan and stayed at the hotel, waiting for his cab to arrive. I had asked the front desk to call my room the minute he walked in the lobby.

"Would you care to give us a description of him?" the cute girl at the front desk had asked me.

"Oh, you'll know. He's French."

She giggled.

When the phone rang in the room, I jumped off the bed.

It was the cute girl calling. "He's here!" More giggles.

I stood at the elevator down the hall from my room, impatiently pushing the call button. The door finally opened and, as I hurriedly stepped inside, I ran headlong into Gérard.

We threw our arms around each other, laughing and kissing.

The doors closed with us still inside. I had always fantasized about being stuck in an elevator with a lover. For some inexplicable reason, the elevator didn't move. For a few blissful minutes, we were sealed off from the world, suspended in space, doing what lovers do.

～

I had champagne on ice back at the room. But we didn't get to that till much later.

Our passion was intense that night. I felt like I hadn't seen Gérard in a year. Our lovemaking was frenzied, as though we were both ravenously consuming a feast that might be taken away. I'm sure the entire tenth floor heard my orgasmic cries that night. I didn't care or even know where I was in that moment. I was floating in a blinding zone of hot white light.

Our sweaty bodies were pressed against each other in the tangled bedsheets, as we caught our breath. Gérard raised up on one elbow, and gently traced the outline of my raw lips with a finger.

"Hello, *chérie*," he whispered.

I smiled. "Hello, my love."

～

We both slept like babies that night.

I awoke to the feel of Gérard's hand moving up between my legs. His fingers stroked me.

I moaned softly, still in the throes of sleep. "I've never been awakened like this," I murmured.

"Do you like it?"

"*Oui.*" I opened my eyes. Gérard was kissing my hair.

I thought about what Alex had said to me, about gifts from the universe. I had no conscious awareness of the secrets of my soul from past incarnations. But I felt divinely guided on this journey that began on the beach, on the day before my 40th birthday, and that had brought me to an old moulin in Giverny.

My breath quickened at Gérard's touch.

"Slowly, slowly," he whispered. "I want you to come slowly. I want you to remember this morning for the rest of our lives."

~

That afternoon, we bundled ourselves up and went for a walk on Michigan Avenue. It was Gérard's first visit to Chicago, but as a scholar of architecture, he knew the landmarks well and the stories of their creators: Louis Sullivan, Raymond Hood, Daniel Burnham. I loved that I was holding the arm of a foreigner who was telling me so much I didn't know about the city I thought I knew so well.

It was the day before Thanksgiving and Chicago was already decorated for Christmas. That surprised Gérard.

"You won't be able to move through the stores here on Friday," I told him. "It's the biggest shopping day of the year. The next biggest shopping day is the day after Christmas, when everyone is back for the big sales or to exchange the presents they didn't like."

The store window decorations were elaborate. The castle-like water tower at Water Tower Place looked like something out of a twinkly fantasyland.

"How would you like to spend Christmas this year?" he asked.

"With you."

He smiled. "Where shall we go?"

"I'll let you decide. Surprise me."

~

The next morning, Gérard and I had a leisurely room-service breakfast.

"This is your last meal until dinner," I told him. "You won't believe the food you'll be consuming today."

Gérard had never experienced an American Thanksgiving. "I've been dreaming about this," he said. "For years." We packed up the bottles of Bordeaux, along with some French chocolates he had brought. I had gotten a pumpkin cheesecake from Eli's, Chicago's version of cheesecake heaven. We decided to take a cab to Alex's apartment in Lincoln Park. It was way too cold to wait for a train.

Alex had moved to Lincoln Park a few months earlier. Carolyn was still at their house in Evanston.

Gérard and I were the first to arrive, except for Alex's sister Beth and her husband who had come in from Milwaukee the night before. Beth had been hard at work in the kitchen. A table of hors d'oeuvres was already prepared, with wine glasses ready to be filled.

Alex gave Gérard a warm welcome and a few minutes later, gave me an approving wink. I could tell he liked The Frenchman. The two of them were uncorking wine bottles, talking about the French grape harvest that fall.

The gang began arriving. It had been almost a year since we'd all been together. The original group of six had grown to nine at one point. Two in the group had married each other, and three others had married "outsiders," leaving me as the singleton, though I sometimes brought my boyfriend-of-the-moment to these gatherings. Our numbers swelled when the babies began arriving. The current nose count of little ones was five, but the eldest wasn't so little anymore. I couldn't believe our firstborn was now 10. He'd soon be a teenager.

I was lost in thought, remembering all the special times we'd shared – the weddings and baby showers, the camping trips, movie nights, homecoming tailgates, and Cubs games at Wrigley Field.

An arm slipped around my shoulder. Gérard kissed my cheek.

"I feel like I'm meeting your family," he said.

"You are."

"They're wonderful."

I smiled at him. "I'm so glad you're here."

"Me, too."

The feast that night was memorable, mostly because of Gérard. He tried everything on the table, relishing the stories everyone had to tell about the food they had brought and the recipes. He had never had cranberries, which he loved, and was amazed to learn they were harvested in bogs. He loved it all – the butterball turkey, chestnut stuffing, candied yams, breaded oysters, giblet gravy, creamed pearl onions, squash casserole, buttermilk biscuits, pecan-pumpkin pie.

As we went around the table saying what we were thankful for, 3-year-old Emma said, "I'm thankful for the mashed potatoes and the butter on top." Gérard quietly said *amen*, which got a big laugh.

Gérard said he was thankful for the day I appeared at the moulin. "It was the luckiest day of my life." A chorus of *here-here* was heard round the table. He turned to me.

"Gérard is my dream come true. I'm so, so grateful," I said with a little quiver in my voice. The women at the table let out a resounding *awwww*.

Alex raised his glass. "To our beloved Kate and her white knight. Welcome, Gérard." Glasses clinked. Gérard was officially one of us.

There was a photo taken that night that is my favorite of all the reunion photos over the years. We're all piled on Alex's big sofa, our bellies full from that incredible meal. I'm sitting at the end curled up next to Gérard. His arm is around me, his head resting on mine. We're both smiling – glowing, actually. I later learned that the most often asked question that evening was: *Have you ever seen Kate so happy?*

The next morning, Gérard and I were waiting on the steps of the Art Institute, the first visitors of the day. The American Impressionist exhibition had opened earlier that week and I knew the galleries would be crowded as the day went on.

It was a bit surreal seeing Robinson's Giverny paintings with Gérard, halfway around the world from the moulin. We knew the scenes so well because we had stood where he had planted his easel.

I said nothing as we entered the gallery where *A Marauder* was on display. Gérard went to it immediately, looking at the wall tag, just as I had. I glanced at the tag again, to see the date – 1891.

Gérard looked at me in surprise. "This is by Robinson."

I nodded. "Have you ever seen it?"

"Never." He looked at it intently for a minute. "There's something familiar about this gate behind her. I wonder if it's the one up the road from the moulin, beyond Theodore Butler's place."

Butler, the groom from Robinson's *The Wedding March*, had lived in a big rambling house on a secluded property behind La Maison Rose, where Isadora Duncan had stayed. Butler had painted a similar gate with a fruit tree blossoming in the garden beyond it.

I didn't say anything to Gérard then about my experience when I first saw the painting several days earlier. Nor did I tell him about Robinson's rumored love child.

I slipped my arm through Gérard's. "She's sweet, isn't she?"

"Adorable." He smiled. "Don't you want to give her a big hug?"

At that moment, I knew for certain that I was in love with Gérard.

~

We spent most of that day at the Art Institute. I showed Gérard my old friends – the paintings I had spent hours gazing at during my student days.

We were looking at Georges Seurat's pointillist master-piece *A Sunday Afternoon on the Island of La Grande Jatte*, with all its synergistic dots of paint.

"When I was growing up in California," I told Gérard, "a lovely woman called The Picture Lady used to come to our classroom once a month. She'd bring a poster of a painting and tell us about the artist and the scene in the painting. I was about 10 years old and had never been to an art museum. But because of The Picture Lady, I developed an appreciation for art."

Gérard smiled at me. I could tell he was smiling at more than my story about The Picture Lady.

"This was the first painting she showed us. She told us that the entire picture was painted with tiny dots. I just couldn't imagine it. On my first visit here, when I was in college, I came to this room first, to see *this* painting. I couldn't believe my eyes. It took my breath away."

He leaned closer to me and whispered, "You, Madame Picture Lady, take my breath away."

We went back to the hotel and made love. I was beginning to feel drugged by the dopamine my brain was secreting. The more we had sex, the more sex I wanted. I'd read somewhere that dopamine, in fact, is the hormone that keeps the human race from going extinct. It enables sexually hyperactive humans to function with amazing clarity despite very little sleep.

I was burning zillions of calories, happily. My jeans were actually feeling a little loose. But my voracious appetite hadn't diminished.

That night, we had Thanksgiving redux in our room. Alex's sister had sent us home with a shopping bag full of leftovers and picnic tableware. We made use of the microwave on top of our mini-fridge where we'd stashed all the perishables. We set our little round corner table with plastic cutlery, poured an oaky California chardonnay into our bathroom glasses and heaped our paper plates with everything in the shopping bag.

Gérard was in hog heaven. "God, these oysters are amazing. They even taste good with cranberries on them." He had given in to the concept that no aesthetic white space is left between food on an American dinner plate. "This all tastes as good as it did last night."

I smiled. My Frenchman was having an American moment. I shared with him the common wisdom about Thanksgiving: "The best part of this meal is the leftovers."

～

I had a little tummy ache when I fell asleep that night. I blamed it on the past 24 hours of binge eating. And I also wanted to blame the binge for the dream I had that night.

But the dream went beyond oysters smothered in cranberries. My experience at the exhibition had unsettled me. The little girl. The voice in my ear. The "wench in the grass," as Alex called her. I couldn't seem to shake it.

My dream that night was horrifying. I was floating in a garden pond, looking up at the mosaic pattern of bright green leaves against a blue sky. The water was warm on my skin. I was naked. I felt so free and uninhibited.

I could hear a man's voice. "*Chérie,*" he said. His voice sounded like Gérard's. The man was standing on a bridge above the pond. I couldn't see his face. Only the backlit silhouette of him, but he appeared to be taller and thinner than Gérard. The man's voice became urgent. "*Chérie*, take my hand." I could see him reaching for me.

It was then I noticed the water around me was turning red. The dream became a jumble of images. I suddenly was underwater. A baby's head was protruding from my vagina. Its little face was blue. I tried to scream, but my lungs filled with water. I reached between my legs, struggling to pull the baby free. Big fish were swimming around my legs, biting the baby. I tried to push my head to the surface, but I was sinking. I had no more air…

I woke up gasping, dripping with sweat. Gérard was holding me. "*Chérie,*" he kept saying. A baby was crying in the room next to ours.

"Gérard, oh god." I could barely breathe. I truly felt like I was drowning.

"Shhh, *chérie*." He gently massaged my diaphragm. "Try to relax."

I started to tell him about the dream.

"Don't talk," he said. "Just breathe. Slowly. That's it. A little deeper. Good."

"Gérard, I was drowning…"

"You're okay, my love. I'm here." He held me close, stroking my damp curls. "Shhh, shhh, shhh," he whispered over and over, trying to lull me back to sleep.

I was afraid to close my eyes. The terror of the dream kept me awake long after Gérard had fallen back to sleep.

~

The next morning, Gérard was eager to take an architectural walking tour of the Loop. It was cold out and I knew the tour would take a couple of hours. I hadn't slept much. I just wasn't up for it. But I wanted him to go. Absolutely, I told him. I'd have a leisurely morning in the room. We'd have lunch together when he got back. Agreed.

Alex called shortly after Gérard left. The minute I heard his voice, I burst into tears. I started telling him about the dream, but didn't get very far.

"Get out of your jammies," he said, "and meet me downstairs in 30 minutes. At that little coffee bar off the lobby."

I took a shower and tried to perk myself up. Alex was already waiting for me when I got downstairs.

My eyes were red and swollen. I couldn't stop crying. He held my hand and listened to the story of the dream, punctuated with my hiccups.

"My sweet Kate." That's all he said for a minute. "You're going down a rabbit hole here, and I want you to know I'm right behind you. You're going to move through this and I'm going to help you, okay?"

I nodded, wanting to believe him. "Is there something wrong with me?"

"There's nothing *wrong* with you." He squeezed my hand. "You are having an extraordinary spiritual experience that defies conventional science perhaps. But as I said to you the other day, open yourself to this. We'll do it carefully, together. Okay?"

He pulled a tissue from his jacket pocket. As I blew my nose, I looked up to see Gérard standing at the entrance to the bar, looking at us.

He walked over to the table in what felt like slow motion. Alex was on his feet, greeting him, shaking his hand.

But Gérard's eyes were on me. "*Chérie*, what's happened?"

"I..." The words got caught in my throat. "I didn't expect you back so soon."

"It's really cold outside. And I was worried about you."

"I'm okay." I knew I was saying all the wrong things. I secretly hoped Alex would rescue me.

"You don't look okay." Gérard sat down next to me and looked up at Alex.

"Kate needs to talk to you, Gérard – she's processing a lot."

"Okay," Gérard said. It was an awkward moment. Gérard was looking at me, waiting for me to speak. But I wanted a little more time alone with Alex.

"Just give me a few more minutes with Alex," I told Gérard.

"Right." Gérard stood up. "See you upstairs."

As Gérard walked away, I looked at Alex. "That didn't go real well, did it?"

Alex sighed. "Do you want me to talk to Gérard, with you?"

I shook my head. "I don't think that would help. Not right now."

We talked for a few minutes about what I should say to Gérard. I knew I needed to be honest with him, but I dreaded his reaction.

"He'll think I'm crazy."

"Are you sure you don't want me to go with you?"

I nodded.

"If you need backup, will you call me?"

"Definitely."

"You're going to be okay, Kate. Try to see the gift in this." Alex leaned over and kissed my forehead. "Come. I'll walk you to the elevator."

~

When I got back to the room, Gérard was staring out the window. He back was rigid, his hands jammed in his pockets. When he heard the door open, he turned to face me, struggling to control his anger.

"What was going on down there?"

"Gérard, this is difficult for me to talk about."

"What is it that you can tell Alex, but not me?"

"Please don't do this."

"Don't do what? What have I done?"

"It's something that happened to me at the moulin. The first night…"

I briefly recounted the story of that night and then told him what happened at the exhibition when I first saw the painting of the little girl with the cherries.

He looked at me incredulously, like I had just told him I had been traveling with space aliens.

I felt myself unraveling. "You think I'm crazy, right?"

"Kate, come on. You're telling me there's a ghost at the moulin who followed you to Chicago and is whispering in your ear at the Art Institute."

"Forget it."

"Forget it? That's asking a lot."

"Enough, Gérard."

"What does Alex say about this?"

"He doesn't think I'm crazy."

"I don't think you're crazy, but…"

"But you don't believe me."

"I don't *understand* this. This is a side of you I haven't seen."

"A side of me? What does that mean?"

"Kate, don't be so defensive."

"How do you expect me to react?" My temper was rising.

"Why were you crying downstairs?"

"Because… " I couldn't tell him about the dream.

"Kate…is Alex an old lover?"'

"*What?*"

"When I saw you both downstairs, I couldn't help but wonder. He's recently separated from his wife. Are there old feelings between you?"

"Alex and I have been friends for a long time."

"Do you have feelings for him?"

"He's one of my oldest and dearest friends."

"Were you ever lovers?"

"Stop asking me that. Don't you trust me to be faithful to you?"

He didn't answer me. My anger was reeling out of control.

"I'm not Pamela!" I shouted at him. As soon as those words flew out of my mouth, I instantly wanted to take them back.

Gérard looked like I just thrown a knockout punch. He actually seemed to wobble a little. He stormed out of the room, slamming the door behind him.

He didn't come back. A half hour later I went looking for him. I found him at the hotel bar, with an empty beer glass in front of him, staring at a college football game on TV.

I sat on the stool next to him. "Gérard, I'm so sorry." My heart sank when he didn't reply. He didn't even look at me. I felt like Coco that first morning at the moulin, after she'd knocked over the ladder and spilled the paint. I just wanted to kiss and make up.

"Alex and I have never been lovers," I said. "We got a little drunk one night and ended up sleeping in the same bed. We woke up the next morning with our clothes on, asking each other what had happened. Apparently, it was nothing memorable. That was 20 years ago."

Gérard looked at me. I saw the flicker of a smile in his eyes. But he said nothing.

I was feeling hormonal and tired and unsettled by the dream. "I didn't get much sleep last night. I'm going upstairs to take a nap." I patted his arm as I slid off the barstool.

Back at the room, I pulled the curtains closed. The sky was gray. Snow was predicted. I undressed and slipped under the covers, my back to the door. A few minutes later, the door opened and then closed softly. I heard Gérard unbuckle his belt. He sat down on the bed, taking off his jeans and shirt. He spooned himself around me, his arm around my middle.

He nuzzled me and said, "Tell me about the phantom."

He listened to the story again. He wasn't judgmental or unkind. He told me he had heard me singing the second night, as he was leaving the moulin after he had walked me back from our dinner at the Baudy.

"I had gone out to the shed to put away some tools and when I came back to the courtyard, I heard you singing. I stood there for a few minutes, listening. You have a lovely voice." He kissed my neck.

We both fell asleep. It was late afternoon when we woke up ravenously hungry. We had eaten most of the Thanksgiving leftovers the night before, so we got dressed and went down to the hotel restaurant.

It was snowing. We had a lovely view of the swirling snowflakes from our table in the dining room. Our conversation steered toward safe topics – the art we had seen, the architectural wonders of Chicago, the crème brûlée we had for dessert.

There's something about the first spat that sadly marks an end to those initial blissful weeks or months of a relationship, which is like a newborn baby – everything about it is perfect and new and unbelievably wondrous. Even toes smell heavenly. Well, at least baby toes smell heavenly.

Gérard and I had had an emotional paper cut over Julie, but this episode had cut to the bone for both of us. In our anger, we railed at each other from two very different places of vulnerability. I was afraid he'd think I was crazy. Alex understood my story because he was a *New York Times* bestselling author-expert on regression therapy. Gérard was an architect, whose handwriting followed the imaginary line of a ruler. I was the loopy one. The girl from California who, for all he knew, read her tea leaves every morning. One day we'd both laugh about his valiant attempt to process my phantom story: *You're telling me there's a ghost at the moulin who followed you to Chicago and is whispering in your ear at the Art Institute.* It makes me laugh even now.

In his logical brain, Gérard was telling himself he could find a tool in his box to tighten my loose bolts. But for him, the potential deal-breaker was my relationship with Alex. In Gérard's cellular memory from his not-so-distant past, he had the very real vision of walking into his London apartment one afternoon, hearing Pamela's moans of passion and then finding her in their bed with Philippe. It would be a long time before Gérard could tell me *that* story: the story of his suicidal thoughts in the days that followed, the fear in his gut that he would never find another woman that he could love as much.

When I appeared at the moulin, he knew his dark days were over, he told me many years later. "You were a blast of sunshine for me."

"And I thought when I met you that your grin could light up a room," I told him.

He sweetly said, "That was reflected light."

After dinner at the hotel in Chicago that night, we went for a short walk. The city was quiet under its blanket of snow. We found a little park decorated with strands of colored lights. Gérard folded me inside his heavy overcoat and kissed me the way he had the first time, at *Le Vivier*. The touch of our lips was tentative and sweet.

We turned a page that night. The story of our early love affair was over. But it wasn't the end of the book. There would be many chapters to come. Deep in my soul, I *knew* that.

~

The next day got off to a rocky start when I received an e-mail from my editor at *ARTnews*, saying he'd like me to stay on in Chicago a few more days to work with the photographer he had assigned for my story about the Terra Foundation collection. He wanted photos of Sonia and others on the staff and needed my input.

I couldn't say no. But the problem was Gérard and I had planned to fly back to Paris together the next day, the Monday after Thanksgiving.

When I told Gérard about the e-mail, he didn't seem to mind at first. But as the day wore on, with him packing and me prepping for my work the next day, there was palpable tension in the air. It seemed hard to believe that only several days earlier, we had been giddy lovers in the elevator.

Our lovemaking that night was nothing like our first night together in that room. The friction of the past few days felt like a whole-body burn. We desperately needed a salve.

The next morning, things got worse.

"When will you be back?" he asked, as he zipped up his suitcase.

"I don't know. Probably later this week." I stood by the bed, still in my pajamas.

He looked unsure.

"I'll call you when I re-book the flight," I said.

"Okay." He kissed me on the cheek.

"Gérard…no." I pulled him toward me and kissed him on the lips.

He ran his hand through my tousled hair. "I'll see you later this week."

The door shut behind him a minute later. It was a horrible good-bye.

～

I called Alex immediately. We met for lunch, at a French bistro near the hotel. His restaurant choice was purposeful. He wanted to remind me what was waiting for me back in Paris. He knew the importance of food in my life.

He knew, too, that I had been starving at the table of the life I'd had in California, especially in the year before I

111

moved to Paris. So he was surprised to hear me say that I was thinking of going to L.A. for a week or so, after I finished my work in Chicago.

"Why?" he asked. Alex was a master of the direct question.

"I've been gone for eight months," I said, counting on my fingers. "I want to see friends. I want a real margarita. I need some time to sit on the beach with the sun on my face. You know how I hate winter weather. I have seasonal adjustment disorder."

"Who diagnosed that?"

"Me."

Alex laughed. "Sweetie pie, you're in the middle of a little crisis. So what happened with Gérard on Saturday? I kept waiting for your call."

"I didn't have a private moment to phone you."

"Was it bad?"

"Oh, yeah. Gérard basically thought – still thinks? – that you and I are old lovers and now that you're splitting from Carolyn, we're going to hook up again."

"Seriously?"

"I understand what's happening here. Gérard was engaged a couple of years ago to an English woman, who was having an affair with his best friend. He found out a few months before the wedding."

"Christ."

"Gérard was living in London then. He moved home to Giverny and bought the moulin, which was a mess. He threw himself into the renovations and redesigned it as a B&B."

"How's it going?"

"It's beautiful. He's focused on what needs to be done and really seems to enjoy the work. And he's had a good first season."

"I'd say he had an amazing first season. He met you." Alex smiled.

"I'm truly happy, Alex. I want this to last. You know how it goes with me. I get to a point in a relationship, and things fizzle. I don't want that to happen with Gérard. I *love* him, Alex."

"I've never heard you say that about anyone. Have you told Gérard this?"

"Not yet."

"Why not?"

"I'm waiting for the right moment."

"Are you waiting for him to say it first?"

"Maybe."

"I think, right now, he needs to hear you say it. Maybe you should skip L.A."

I shook my head. "No. I need some time to stare at the sea. It's how I make all my big decisions."

"Well, okay then. Put me on speed dial."

9

Before I left Chicago, I had another chance to meet with Sonia Hillard at the Terra Foundation. The exhibition was drawing big crowds. She was thrilled and thanked me for the article I had written, which was coming out that week, about the American artists in Giverny. My editor had sent her an advance copy.

"I see you're a fan of Theodore Robinson, too," she said.

"I am. I've had the pleasure of staying at the old moulin and feel I've walked in his footsteps."

"I was in Giverny when the new owner was starting work on the moulin."

"He's done an amazing job. In fact, he was just here in Chicago last week. We saw the exhibition together last Friday."

"Really? What did he think?"

"He loved it. We felt like we were walking through Giverny a hundred years ago. He knows Robinson's paintings well, but there was one he had never seen – the little girl by the gate with the cherries."

"Yes. *A Marauder,*" she said. "Getting that painting was a coup."

"Where did it come from?"

"A private collection. The owner demanded strict anonymity. Sorry, my lips are zipped."

"Do you know who the little girl is?"

"She's a bit of a mystery. Like Marie."

"Could she be the love child?"

She smiled. "I've wondered that myself."

After the *ARTnews* photographer took the photos he needed of Sonia in her office, she said to me, "If you have a few minutes, I'd like to show you some images in our photo archives."

The room looked like the stacks of a library, with rows of tall shelves. But the "books" were actually cases holding vintage photographs, some of them albumen prints and cyanotypes like those that Robinson had taken.

Sonia pulled a case from a shelf and took it to a layout table surrounded by stools.

"Have a seat," she said. "I have a treat for you."

She carefully opened the case. She put on white protective cloth gloves before she pulled out a sleeve of photos layered with archival tissue.

The first image was of a man, almost in profile, sitting in what looked to be a rattan chair. He had short hair, angular facial features accentuated by a prominent brow line, and a trimmed goatee and moustache. He wore a dark suit. The jacket was buttoned nearly to the neck, revealing only the knot of a tie and a starched shirt collar. In his lap, he held a sketchpad with one hand. A pencil was poised in the other.

Sonia smiled. "*This* is our Theodore."

The photo bore the caption "Theodore Robinson Sketching in France," but there was no date.

Everything about him was familiar. He looked healthy in this photo. I could see the line of his strong lean thigh through the fabric of his trousers. I looked closely at his face and smiled. Even though the image was faded and a bit fuzzy, I could sense the fire in his eyes.

Sonia then carefully removed three photos taken by Robinson and laid them on the table. "And this…is Marie."

I recognized one immediately – it was the pose Robinson had used as the basis for *The Layette*, with Marie sewing, seated on a wooden ladder-back chair next to a tree.

I had seen it both in the museum in Giverny and at the Chicago exhibition. But based on what I had read, I thought it was the only known photo of Marie. But there on the table were two others. Both appeared to be in the same location, in an unkempt garden. One image captured Marie with her head bent over her work – not in profile as Robinson typically painted her, but at an angle from the front. The other photo is a profile shot of her sitting in front of a gnarled fruit tree with a trunk bent at a near 90-degree angle. Marie's hair is swept up in a bun. She's in country dress, wearing a skirt, a sleeveless vest with a gathered neckline, and a white blouse with elbow-length sleeves. All three images were dated 1892.

"Do you know the location of this garden?" I asked.

"Not precisely. Robinson wrote in his diary of a house in the village where a Boston artist named Mariquita Gill and her mother stayed. He mentions it as the setting for *The Layette*. But I've not been able to pinpoint the property."

Sonia showed me another version of Robinson's photo for *The Layette* that he had marked with gridlines. "He often drew gridlines on his photos to help him transfer the image to the canvas, which he'd also mark with gridlines. If you look closely at the finished painting, you'll see a hint of the grid in places."

"Why did he work this way, do you think?"

"Partly because he was a draftsman at heart. In his 20s, he worked as a mural painter for John La Farge and Prentice Treadwell, so he learned to compose a scene with precision. But also, his health kept him from working long hours outdoors. His photographs enabled him to capture a moment and then embellish it in the studio."

"Did he ever travel to other parts of Europe?"

"He was drawn to Italy and the Mediterranean coast. But his health was always an issue. He toured northern Italy in 1878 – and the trip nearly killed him. Robinson had a vibrant soul, but physically, he was not a hale and hearty man."

"Did he and Marie write to each other?" I asked.

"Supposedly, they corresponded when he returned to the U.S. each winter. He didn't spend the winters in France because of his health."

"What happened to the letters?"

"Another mystery. They've never been found."

Gérard called that night. He was back in Giverny after a long trip home. He sounded exhausted.

"How are you?" he asked.

"I've had a busy couple of days. But I'll be wrapping things up tomorrow."

"Have you booked your flight yet?" he asked.

I took a breath, steeling myself for what I had to say. "I'm going to L.A. for a week or so."

He was quiet for a moment. "Why?"

"I'm a four-hour flight away. I haven't been home in eight months. I want to see friends and chill out."

"Chill out?"

"I want to relax. Go for walks on the beach."

I thought the line had gone dead.

"Gérard?"

"I'm here. How long will you stay?"

I hated myself in that moment. But I felt like I was back in that horrible dream, trying to push my mouth through the surface of the pond to gulp a little air. I couldn't breathe life back into this relationship right now. Not when I could barely breathe myself.

"I don't know, Gérard. I don't know."

"Please don't do this, Kate. We'll work this out. Please come home."

I didn't speak, nor did he. At a dollar-a-minute, we couldn't hang on like this too long.

"I love you, Kate." His voice was raw. "Please come home."

And then he clicked off.

～

I was sobbing by the time Alex answered his phone.

We met for dinner that evening at the same French bistro. Alex wasn't giving up on his strategy of appealing to my sense of reason through my taste buds.

We sat at a table by the window. A happy-looking couple walked by, which pushed me to the brink of tears – again.

"He said he *loved* me, Alex."

"And why is that so upsetting?" Alex has a way of giving you a bug-eyed look when he's near the limit of his patience. "You love him, yes? This is great news. What's the problem?"

"I should have said *I love you* first, like you said."

"Holy shit, Kate."

The waiter approached and asked if we'd like to order an appetizer.

"We'll both have the escargot," Alex said.

"I hate escargot."

"You had it for lunch two days ago." Alex's eyes were bugging out even more. "What would you like, my sweet peanut?"

"I'll have the oysters."

"She'll have the oysters. I'll have the escargot."

"Wine with that?" the waiter asked.

"What would you recommend?" Alex asked, looking at the wine list.

"Perhaps a glass of the Meursault," the waiter suggested.

"Make that a bottle. I need to anesthetize myself."

The waiter smiled and hurried off.

"Alex, I'm sorry."

"Please tell me you're just PMS-ing."

"*Alex…*"

"No worries, my dear. So are you flying tomorrow to L.A. – or Paris?"

"L.A."

"Are you convinced this is the best plan of action?"

"No."

"You know you're making *me* a little crazy. I'm up to about a nine right now."

The waiter reappeared with the wine. He apparently sensed an urgent need.

Alex looked up at him, like a saint looking to heaven hoping for a divine blessing. "Just bring two straws."

I burst out laughing. So did Alex. He was near tears he was laughing so hard.

The waiter filled our glasses. Alex raised his. "To our mental health or lack of it."

"Cheers, my darling friend."

~

I got on a plane the next day for L.A. It was 80 degrees when we touched down at LAX. I was ecstatic.

For three days, I ate Mexican food and drank margaritas. Nothing remotely French. I didn't go near a baguette or a croissant, though I caved in on Day 2 bought a bag of French Roast at Starbucks. I was trying to find my emotional center.

I laughed with friends and met my old boyfriend for lunch. I sat through the entire meal wondering how we had spent two years together, even if it was off and on. After lunch that day, I drove up to Malibu to my favorite beach – the same one where I had taken that fateful walk on the day before I turned 40.

I watched the waves make foamy scallops on the wet sand. I let the icy cold water burn my feet. I didn't have the energy or spirit to do a cartwheel, even a pathetic one. I stood looking at the distant horizon line, squinting to see some kind of sign. Like that green flash of light that appears just before sunset. A flock of pelicans flew by. They weren't carrying a banner from their beaks saying *Kate, go back to Paris.*

But on the beach that day, I didn't need a bolt from heaven to tell me that my pre-destined path led to France. Only eight months earlier, I had stood on this same spot, opening my arms to the universe, shaking loose the invisible nets I had gotten myself caught in. I'd had an amazing journey since then and had met the man of my dreams.

So why was I thinking of *not* spending Christmas with him? By reason of temporary insanity, I told myself.

Alex had been calling me twice a day. He'd call first thing in the morning, to make sure I was out of bed. And then he called at bedtime to see how the day had gone. "I'm okay," I told him on the evening of Day 3. "I'm not having bad dreams. I'm not thinking about what happened in Chicago. I think I've crawled out of the rabbit hole."

"I'm glad, Kate." I could hear the relief in his voice. "How are you feeling about Gérard?"

"I miss him terribly."

"Have you heard from him?"

"No."

"No e-mails?"

"Nothing."

"So...what's your plan?"

"My friends want me to stay for Christmas. They're planning a big New Year's Eve party. That might be fun."

"Are you going to tell Gérard you'll be staying?"

"That would be the kind thing to do."

"Yes, it would."

"Alex..."

"What, sweetie."

"I want to be with Gérard."

"What's stopping you?"

"What if he doesn't want to see me again?"

"I don't think that's likely, do you? He's probably worried you don't want to see him again."

"I'll book my flight and call him when I get back to Paris. How does that sound?"

"That sounds reasonable."

Two days later, I boarded a flight for Paris. I talked to Alex from the lounge at the gate and thanked him for all his moral support.

"Let me know how it goes," he said.

"I'm nervous, Alex."

"Don't be – you know he loves you."

I said that line over and over on the flight to Paris. *You know he loves you.*

We touched down at Charles De Gaulle the next morning. It was a gray, wet day. I hadn't slept much on the flight. I was looking forward to a long sleep in my own little bed.

I got my bag and cleared customs. The doors opened to that hall where families and limo drivers wait. I sometimes feel very alone when I walk that gauntlet, knowing no one is waiting for me.

I was almost to the door of the terminal when I heard a familiar voice say, "*Mademoiselle,* may I help you with your bag?"

I turned around in disbelief.

Gérard smiled at me. "Welcome home, *chérie.*"

"My god. How did you know?"

He chuckled as he hugged me. "You're here. That's all that matters."

~

On the ride to Giverny that morning, Gérard confessed everything. Alex had been keeping him apprised of my movements.

"How did he get in touch with you?"

"He found the number for the moulin online. The first time he called, I must admit I was stunned. It was the day after I got back. He told me he was going to be calling you every day while you were in L.A. I felt better, knowing you weren't at loose ends. He had hoped you'd come back to Paris, but he thought it was important for you to have some time in L.A. I understood that. But it was hard for me."

"I'm sorry for what I've put you through."

He reached over and squeezed my hand, like he did that night after Madame Mallery's party. "We're going to be okay."

I squeezed his hand back. "We're going to be just fine."

~

It had started to rain by the time we got to the moulin.

Gérard quickly got my bags inside. Coco bounded to the front door to greet me. I bent down to rub her head and give her a kiss. Her tail wagged wildly.

"She's missed you, too." Gérard patted her back.

Gérard and I stood in the entryway, really looking at each other for a moment, with dear Coco lying at our feet. Gérard seemed so tired. Our brief separation had taken a toll.

"You look wonderful," he said. "California agreed with you."

"The weather was great."

He stroked my cheek. "You got some sun."

"I had a nice afternoon on the beach."

"And now you've come back to this," he said, looking out at the rain.

I slipped my arms around his waist. "No. I've come back to this."

He pulled me close. "I thought I'd lost you, Kate. Thank god for Alex."

I smiled. "You've changed your tune."

"He's a great guy. We had some good talks."

"About me?"

He grinned. "Yes, about you. But we also talked a lot about Pamela and what I've not been dealing with."

"I'm glad to hear that."

"I want to make this work, Kate. Whatever it takes. I want to understand what *you're* dealing with. Alex explained a lot to me."

"I'm much better. That walk on the beach did me a lot of good."

He kissed me. Thunder rumbled outside. I felt a hormonal bolt of lightning go through me. The thrill was back.

~

"Are you hungry?" Gérard asked, as he brought plates and glasses to the dining table.

"I'm starving. I hate airline food."

He smiled. "This will fill you up so you'll have a nice nap this afternoon."

He had made soup and a quiche and had gotten a big *boule* from Henri. After the first sip of Gérard's favorite Bordeaux, I knew I was home.

We went upstairs after lunch to *my* room with the fairy-tale bed.

"Would you like me to let you sleep?" he asked, putting my suitcase on a bench by the bed.

"No."

He laughed. "You must be exhausted."

"I want to fall asleep in your arms."

We quickly undressed. A rollicking storm was raging at that point. The panes of the big window rattled as we dove under the covers.

Kate, Kate, he murmured over and over. His hands caressed my body as though he had never touched it before.

My climax was incredible. I felt like I was in the curl of a rising wave that was swelling to dizzying heights.

As the water cascaded over the paddle wheel below us, I let myself tumble into a hidden world. It was still a mystery to me then, but I wasn't frightened of it. It was my secret place where I felt safe – and very much loved.

10

Gérard and I had a lovely Christmas together at the moulin. We spent Christmas Eve with his parents and older brother, who were pleased to meet me. Gérard's parents lived in a lovely home at the edge of the village, hidden behind a stone wall. I could imagine the garden in spring, with the flowering pear and apple trees. I was addicted to the jam his mother made from the bounty of her little orchard.

As we walked back to their house from Christmas Eve mass at the village church, Gérard's brother Jean-Luc was beside me. He leaned close to me and said, "We are so happy you have come into Gérard's life."

I smiled at him. "I am, too."

Christmas Day was quiet. Gérard and I lingered in the fairy-tale bed that morning. Gérard had strung twinkle lights on the wrought-iron canopy and had hung a sprig of mistletoe above the headboard. His playful spirit had returned.

In bed that morning, we opened our presents to each other. I gave Gérard a hefty picture book about the architecture of Chicago, which he loved. He gave me a beautiful oil painting a local artist had done of the moulin. In the foreground was the little bridge.

"You can hang this in your apartment and feel you are here," he said.

"My heart will always be here."

The greatest gift of that Christmas was knowing that my heart had found a home.

～

I've never liked January. There's the letdown from the holidays. Mundane tasks loom – like putting away decorations and doing year-end tax accounting. Dreary weather depresses me. I wasn't kidding when I told Alex I had seasonal adjustment disorder.

I felt pretty confident in my self-diagnosis as I sloshed through puddles on my way to a woman's clinic in Paris on a cold gray January morning. It was time for my annual physical. I hadn't yet seen a doctor in France. Although I had a command of basic French, my medical vocabulary was pretty thin. The clinic was highly regarded in Paris, so I hoped there'd be staff who spoke English if I needed a translator.

The waiting area was bright with gorgeous artwork, which lifted my spirits. I sat down next to an elegantly dressed woman who wore a designer silk scarf wrapped around her head. She had artfully tied the ends of the scarf into a twist. And then I noticed that under carefully drawn pencil lines, her eyebrows and eyelashes were missing.

I took a health magazine from the coffee table and tried to concentrate on an article about dietary guidelines for women over 40. I still had trouble seeing myself in that demographic.

A nurse approached the woman with the scarf. In French, she apologized for the wait and told her the doctor would see her shortly.

The woman replied in French. There was something about her voice that was familiar. I stole another glance at her. It took a second, but then I realized: The woman was Madame Mallery.

I knew she had sensed my attention. After the nurse walked away, Madame Mallery looked directly at me. "Do I know you?"

My stomach went into a twist like the one on her scarf. "We've met. At a party at your home in Giverny."

"I give many parties."

"It was last September. I was with Gérard Marchand."

Her eyes were boring holes into me. "You're the magazine writer."

"Yes. Kate Morgan. It's nice to see you again. But maybe the setting could be a little better?"

She was quiet for a moment. "I'm braced for bad news today."

"I'm so sorry."

"I have one of the best doctors in France."

"Don't give up hope."

"That's all I have." Madame Mallery managed a faint smile.

A nurse walked into the reception area and approached me, asking my name.

As I stood to follow her, I impulsively reached into my bag and took out a business card. "If there's anything I can do for you, Madame Mallery, please call me. I'd be happy to help in any way I can."

She took the card, but seemed puzzled by my kindness. "*Merci*," she said.

~

I followed the nurse down a corridor. She opened the door of a bathroom and pointed to a stack of cups on a shelf above the toilet. So far, the drill was the same.

I hadn't been waiting long when a young female doctor entered the examining room. "I'm Dr. Anderssen," she said, extending her hand. "I'm pleased to meet you, Kate." She had a lovely smile.

I was so relieved she spoke English. I had requested a female doctor and was delighted she was about my age. She told me she was Swedish and had done her residency in the States. She had married a Frenchman, explaining how she had ended up in Paris.

She asked what had brought me to Paris, so I shared the short version of my story. She checked over my health history form and asked a few questions. My mother had died of breast cancer 12 years earlier, when she was in her mid-60s.

"I'd like you to have a routine mammogram today so that we have a baseline. Have you had a mammogram before?" she asked.

"Yes, two years ago. Everything was fine."

"Are your menstrual cycles regular?"

"Not so much this past year," I said. "I sometimes go six to eight weeks without a period, but I start having cramps much sooner. I feel like my body is trying to have a period, though nothing happens."

"When was your last period?"

I had to think a minute. "In early November."

"This may be the new normal for you. But we can talk about options if the prolonged onset is making you uncomfortable."

She slipped her stethoscope under my gown and listened to my heart. "We'll check your hormone levels. You have a long way to go before menopause, but changes start happening in your 40s. Take a deep breath for me...and again."

She asked me to lie back on the table and put my right arm above my head. I flinched when she began palpitating my right breast.

"Are your breasts normally tender?"

"Before a period, yes."

"Isn't it fun being a woman?" she asked.

She gently examined the other breast. "Everything feels fine. You can schedule the mammogram at your convenience. I'll give you the form."

She buzzed for the nurse, who came into the room with my urine-test results.

Dr. Anderssen studied the printout. "Well this is interesting." She looked up at me. "I hope this is good news."

"What?"

"You're pregnant."

~

I don't really remember the Metro ride back to Saint-Germain-des-Prés that day. My body felt heavy as I walked up the stairs to my apartment. I shed my clothes and got under the bedcovers. I closed my eyes and stroked my belly. A baby was growing inside me.

I was elated, but still stunned. Dr. Anderssen thought I was about seven weeks along. Gérard and I almost always used protection. But I remembered the day after he had arrived in Chicago. He had slowly brought me to a climax that morning and in the last moments, we had coupled so we could come together. He wasn't wearing a condom.

I suddenly felt so maternal. I thought about all the reunions of my college friends as the little ones had come into the fold. I was an auntie to them. I'd cuddle them and play with them, wistfully wanting to be a mommy someday.

I thought about telling Gérard that night. I hadn't really considered that he wouldn't think it was wonderful news. In the back of my mind, though, I had a gnawing thought: As a couple, were we ready for this? Our relationship was still so new and we had barely recovered from our big upset in Chicago. But we weren't young. Gérard was 45 and I was statistically in the age group in which pregnancy problems loom large. Regardless of what was in the back of my mind, my heart believed this baby was a blessing.

Gérard would be coming to Paris for the weekend the next day. I decided to tell him in person. That would give me a day to embrace the idea of being blessedly with child.

Gérard called about 7, as was his habit when we weren't together. He'd had a long day, installing a new plumbing system in the gatehouse. He'd wrap things up in the morning and would be in Paris by late afternoon.

"How was your day?" he asked.

"Great," I said.

"How did your visit to the clinic go?"

"Fine."

"Everything ok?"

I had been so tempted to blurt out *I'm pregnant!* "Everything's fine." I was beaming.

I made myself a healthy dinner. I went to bed and watched a movie. It was raining. I loved hearing the sound of raindrops on the metal rooftop. I fell asleep thinking all was right with the world.

I awoke at about 3 a.m. doubled up with pain. I ran to the bathroom and threw up. A violent chill went through me and then I was suddenly sweating. The pain in my abdomen cut like a knife. I sat on the toilet as blood clots fell into the toilet.

I knew it was a miscarriage.

Sobbing, I held my belly and rocked back and forth on the toilet.

I didn't sleep. The bleeding was heavy. I used towels to soak up the blood that was draining out of me. By morning, I knew I had to get to the clinic. I called a cab. On my way down the stairs, I thought I was going to pass out.

I had called ahead to let Dr. Anderssen know I was coming. She was waiting for me when I arrived and had a gurney ready for me.

She held my arm as an orderly pushed me down a corridor to a small operating theater. "I'm so sorry," she said. "Don't be frightened. We'll take good care of you."

She explained that she would be performing a D&C – dilation and curettage – a procedure that would clear the uterus of fetal tissue. This would staunch the blood flow, she told me. I was barely comprehending what she was saying. I had already lost a lot of blood.

I woke up an hour later in the recovery area. Dr. Anderssen was at my side. I was still woozy from the anesthetic. I tried to focus on her blurred face. "I didn't get to tell him." I started to cry.

I felt a warm rush up my arm and quickly fell into a deep sleep.

I woke up later in a patient room. At first, I didn't know where I was. A nurse was pumping up a blood pressure cuff. My arm felt like it was going to explode.

Someone was stroking my hair. I looked up to see Gérard.

"I'm here, *chérie*." He leaned over and kissed my forehead.

"I'm so sorry." My words were slurred.

"Shhh, my love." He pulled a chair next to the bed, so that I could see his face.

"You're so handsome," I said, feeling like the words weren't coming out of my mouth.

"Flattery will get you anything you want from me." He held my hand and whispered, "I love you, Kate."

"I love you, too, Gérard."

⁓

I spent the night in the hospital. Gérard stayed in the room with me, dozing in a chair. I woke up in the wee hours, crying in my sleep. Gérard crawled into bed with me and held me close.

Before Dr. Anderssen discharged me the next morning, she came in to see me. Apparently, she had already spoken with Gérard. She assured me that the procedure had gone well. She wanted to see me in two weeks. She looked at us both, "No intercourse before then."

She gave me some supplements she wanted me to take and asked me if I had any questions.

I could barely say the words. "Will I be able to get pregnant again?"

"Nothing has happened in the past 24 hours that will prevent that," she said.

⁓

When Gérard and I got back to the apartment that morning, he made me a light breakfast.

The reality of the past 24 hours was a living nightmare. I desperately wanted it to be just a dream. I wanted to be having breakfast that morning with the father of our baby.

But the baby had been sucked away.

"Okay, you're off to bed," Gérard said as he cleared the breakfast dishes. "I'm under strict doctor's orders to watch over you."

Gérard got into bed next to me. What he said to me next surprised me. "That morning in Chicago when we were making love..." he said. "It was so strange, but I *imagined* the child you and I might conceive. I *wanted* a baby. I saw us as parents."

Tears streamed down my face. *Would they ever stop*, I wondered.

"But it was too soon for us," he said. "Look at all the stress we've had since then." He kissed me gently. "I love you with all my heart, Kate. God willing, we'll have another child someday."

In my little bed that day, Gérard cradled me in his arms, as we both wept for the child who wouldn't be ours.

11

At my two-week check-up, Dr. Anderssen said I had healed well. Gérard was there with me. She advised us to use protection. She told me, "I want you to have a couple of cycles before you try getting pregnant again, if that's your wish. Your body has had a big shock."

She looked empathetically at us both. "Are the two of you okay, considering all that's happened? There are some wonderful counselors on staff here."

Gérard and I smiled at each other. We had been skyping with Alex.

"We have a dear friend who's a psychologist, who has been helping us through this," Gérard said.

"Good," Dr. Anderssen said. "Kate, you're a healthy woman. First pregnancies often spontaneously abort. It doesn't mean you won't have a positive outcome the next time." She smiled at me. "Don't blame yourself for this. It's nature's way. The embryo wasn't viable or didn't imbed properly. You did nothing to make this happen."

I nodded. I could feel a lump swelling in my throat.

"In the next few weeks, schedule that mammogram so we'll have that taken care of." She handed me the form. "I'd like to see you again in a month."

"Thank you so much for your kindness to us," I said.

She took my hand in hers. "I hope to see you both again in happy circumstances."

"Thank you, Dr. Anderssen." Gérard shook her hand. "We'll be back."

~

Gérard and I had had some good news. Alex was coming to London in March to promote his new book. He had added a week to his itinerary and wanted to see us. We insisted that he spend some time with us at the moulin.

Alex was delighted. "Will I get to meet the phantom?" he had asked during a skype call.

Gérard laughed. "We'll see what we can do."

"Stop! Both of you." I pretended to be offended.

Gérard kissed my cheek. "*Chérie*, we love you."

Alex had helped us through our dark days after the miscarriage. It was Gérard who had called him on skype, the second day after I came home from the hospital.

I was in bed when Gérard placed the call to him. I could see him sitting on the sofa in the next room. When Alex appeared on the screen, Gérard's face lit up. I realized how they had bonded during my rogue trip to California. My heart ached a little less in that moment, knowing the two men I loved most in the world were fast becoming good friends.

Alex was devastated when Gérard told him the news. Like Gérard, he had the double shock of hearing about the pregnancy and the loss of it, all in one sentence. Gérard later told me how he broke down in Dr. Anderssen's office, after she told him the news.

"My god, Gérard…I'm so sorry. How is she?" Alex asked.

I imagined he was re-living his own nightmare, when Carolyn miscarried.

"She's resting, but she's awake. Hold on…"

Gérard brought the laptop to me. I had propped myself up with pillows. When I saw Alex's face, I started to cry.

"Oh sweetie…" Alex said. "I wish skype had a hug button. How are you?"

I suddenly felt like an animal that had just been pierced by an arrow to the heart. The wail that came out of me was from the animal core of me. I had seen a *National Geographic* film about wild beasts grieving over their dead young. I had this image burned in my mind of a female lion, dragging around her dead cub. She'd lay in the grass next to the lifeless ball of fur, crying in pain.

Every day for a week, Gérard and I talked to Alex. As a psychologist, Alex's advice is a blend of ethos, pathos and logos. He speaks to you from his learned wisdom as a doctor of psychology, but in a way that addresses your emotional and mental state on a deeply personal level.

"This is a raw emotional experience, Kate," he assured me one day when I asked why I couldn't stop crying. "Your hormones are raging and your body is confused because of the mixed signals your brain is transmitting. You're in shock. Don't try to see the logic in what's happening to you right now. Just know that this is a process. Hang in there, sweetie. Better days are coming. You must believe that."

As Alex had predicted, slowly the days got better.

Those were tender days for Gérard and me. We learned to experience intimacy without intercourse. It was difficult at first, not to be able to indulge our passion without him inside me. But we learned other ways to bring each other pleasure. Gérard treated me like a fragile egg, which actually heightened my desire and my physical sensations.

I desperately wanted a child with him. I wanted us to begin a life together as a family. It wasn't too late for us. But I knew that time was marching on. *Patience, patience,* I told my impatient self.

I thought of my own parents who had given up hope of having a child. They conceived me when my mother was in her early 40s. I truly was a miracle to them. I missed them so much. I had lost them both before I turned 30.

My mother used to tell me when I'd be on the rebound after a breakup: "Honey, there's a man out there looking for you, too. You're going to find each other someday and it's going to be wonderful."

Mom had been right. Gérard and I had finally found each other. That's what really mattered. We already were so very blessed.

~

I got a surprise call one day, about a month after my miscarriage.

"Miss Morgan?" the woman said. "It's Madame Mallery."

I almost dropped the phone. "*Bonjour, Madame.*"

"I'm comfortable speaking English," she said. I sensed she couldn't bear my Americanized pronunciation of French.

"Of course," I said. I had a lot to learn about this formidable woman.

"I have a proposition for you – a writing project that may interest you. Would you be available to come to my apartment the day after tomorrow at 11 a.m.?"

"Yes, I'd be happy to."

"Good. Let me give you the address. 220 Rue de Rivoli."

Rue de Rivoli. The chicest address in Paris.

~

I arrived 10 minutes early and stood outside the building, taking in Madame Mallery's neighborhood. Rue de Rivoli is one of the grandest boulevards in Paris, lined with the arcaded façades of luxurious shops and five-star hotels. High-end apartments overlook the boulevard, with a sweeping view of the Louvre and the Tuileries Gardens.

When I had told Gérard about meeting Madame Mallery at the clinic, he told me she had had breast cancer a few years earlier. "She seemed to rebound quickly, as is her way," he said. "I'm so sorry to hear this." When I told him about the call I had gotten from her, he said, "I must send her a note."

A few minutes before 11, I approached the doorman at Madame Mallery's apartment building. He had been expecting me and pointed his white-gloved hand to a wrought-iron encased elevator that looked like a birdcage at the far end of the marble-clad foyer.

A uniformed elevator man nodded when I said I was seeing Madame Mallery. He closed the elevator car's inner accordion gate and pressed the button for the top floor. Of course, Madame Mallery lived in the penthouse.

I was stunned when I got off the elevator to see a private security guard at her front door. He was armed, with a large handgun in his holster. He asked my name and wanted to see my ID. He then rang the bell. A young maid in a starched uniform opened the door.

She greeted me and showed me to a sitting room off the grand salon. The salon's décor was opulent – dazzling chandeliers; enormous oil paintings; a Chinoise porcelain vase with a spray of exotic fresh flowers, sitting on a Napoleon-era table trimmed with ormolu embellishments; and endless swags of luxurious brocades framing the immense windows that looked out on the Tuileries Gardens.

Madame Mallery was waiting for me in the adjoining sitting room, comfortably appointed with two sofas, facing each other, with overstuffed down cushions. She was reading the morning paper. She wore a black cashmere shawl, pinned with a ruby brooch, over a high-necked burgundy sweater. Her black wool trousers were slit at the ankles, revealing black-lace stockings and her Audrey Hepburnstyle Ferragamo flats. Her makeup was heavy – her brow and eyeliner pronounced. A paisley scarf wrapped her head.

"Good morning, Madame Mallery," I said warmly, extending my hand.

She didn't stand, but shook my hand politely. I wondered if I already had made a *faux pas* by assuming she'd want to shake hands.

"Good morning, Miss Morgan. Please sit down," she said, motioning to the sofa opposite hers.

On the glass coffee table between us were art magazines and a lovely floral arrangement.

"What beautiful flowers," I said.

Her expression hardened. "They're from Gérard."

"Really?" I didn't realize he had intended to send flowers with the note he planned to write.

"I assume you told him you would be seeing me – and apparently you told him of my health problems?"

"Only that I had seen you at the clinic and that you had called me a few days ago, asking to meet."

"How many other people have you told?"

"No one." I suddenly felt this was going to be a very short meeting.

"Are you so intimate with Gérard that you share the details of every phone call you receive?"

"Madame Mallery, I didn't come here today to talk about Gérard – with all due respect," I said.

"If you are going to work for me, I will demand absolute discretion."

"Work for you?"

Madame Mallery and I were squaring off. I was recalling Gérard's advice about dealing with her and Pierre Gaston: *Don't let them bowl you over.*

Madame Mallery sized me up for a moment. "I've asked you here today to discuss a writing project that would pay you a sizeable sum, if I were to hire you. What we will discuss must never leave here. I will ask you to sign a contract that will state this explicitly. No pillow talk about this with Gérard."

Furious, I stood up. "I think we're finished here, Madame Mallery."

She looked shocked. She was accustomed to stepping way over the line, but wasn't used to being blown back for her rude behavior.

"I see you have a temper," she said.

"I have no tolerance for insults." I felt an inch taller. I'd found my backbone.

She rang for the maid. "Charlotte, please bring us some tea. Chamomile for Miss Morgan."

I looked at the maid. "I don't drink tea. I'd like a *café au lait*, please. Easy on the milk."

The bewildered maid looked at Madame Mallery, who said, "As she wishes, Charlotte." Then to me, she said quietly, "Miss Morgan, please won't you have a seat? Let's begin again."

∽

Despite our rough start, the remainder of our hour together struck a more amicable tone. Madame Mallery explained that she wanted to compile her diaries and personal correspondence in a memoir-style book, with photographs. "I'm not equal to writing a narrative for this," she told me. "I would rely on you for that, based on our conversations. You're a journalist. I think you would be skilled at weaving the threads of this together, *oui*?"

"Yes, I could do that."

"You will come here three mornings a week and will work here in this room. I'll provide you with a computer to work on. Initially, your job will be to cull excerpts from letters and diary entries and transcribe them on the computer. I will not be meeting with you at every session, but I will review your work and make comments and suggestions so that you better understand what I'm looking for."

"Are you planning to publish this?" I asked.

"Certainly not. This is for my son, Thierry – my only child. I want him to know the story of my life."

She waited for my reaction and then said, "You know he and Gérard are friends."

I remembered the night of her party when I asked Gérard how he knew her. "Yes, he mentioned that to me once," I told her.

"I will insist on a pledge of secrecy," she said emphatically.

I nodded.

The fee she was offering was staggering. I wouldn't have to write another article for months.

"Are you willing to take this on?" she asked.

"Yes."

"Do you think we can work together?" Bluntness was Madame Mallery's hallmark.

"With constructive guidance from you, I think I can deliver what you want."

"Good." She reached for a folder that had been sitting on the sofa next to her. Inside was a one-page contract. "Look this over today. If you're in agreement, please sign it and bring it with you to our next meeting. We will begin on Monday."

I started reading the terms of the contract.

"Take it with you and think about it," she said. "But if you decide to decline the offer, I'd like to know that by tomorrow. Please let me know either way."

I put the folder in my bag and once again, stood up. Madame Mallery didn't stand, but she offered her hand.

"I hope to see you Monday," she said.

"I will let you know tomorrow," I replied.

Charlotte, the maid, appeared at the doorway, ready to show me out.

~

Gérard was at the apartment when I got back from my interview with Madame Mallery. The story of our meeting tumbled out of me.

"I can't believe it." Gérard was incensed that she pinned me to the wall about my relationship with him. "I'll never send her flowers again."

We were sitting at my kitchen table. "I would greatly appreciate that." I patted his hand, smiling at his indignation.

Gérard read over the contract. "What do you want to do?"

"It's a lot of money."

Gérard agreed. "But she's very demanding. I know. I worked for her. You'll have to stand your ground with her." He loved that I almost walked out on her. "You've put her on notice that you're not a pushover. That's good. But she'll test you – over and over."

He called an attorney friend of his and faxed him a copy of the contract. The attorney said it was straightforward, but pointed to the language that said any indiscretion would be an actionable offense. "Kate can't discuss this project with *anyone*," he told Gérard. "If she does, Madame Mallery could take her to court."

"*Chérie*, it's up to you," Gérard said to me. "I can't imagine that she has horribly dark secrets. She's accustomed to guarding her privacy. Look at the way she lives – with an armed guard at the door. No one intrudes on her world. She wants this book to be a gift to Thierry. What an extraordinary gift. And she's entrusting you with it."

"This is why I love you – one of the many reasons I love you," I told him.

He smiled at me. "How do you mean?"

"You have such clear vision, especially when things seem blurry. You focus on what's important and just shove the rest aside. I'm not so good at that."

"Yes, but you see beauty in the blurriness that I miss."

I kissed him on the cheek. "We're a good team."

I signed the contract and called Madame Mallery the next morning to tell her I would see her on Monday. She sounded pleased.

My first session with her went well, but I could see after an hour had passed that she was fatigued. She left me to read a diary from her early travels with her husband.

"It's not a sex diary," she assured me, which made me smile. I couldn't imagine Madame Mallery writing tales from her *boudoir*.

Before she excused herself, she told me that she'd like me to note, on a tablet she had provided, excerpts I thought would be appropriate for the book. "I want to capture the romance and setting of our travels," she said. "I want to include the names of our friends and what we did together and talked about. I'm not publishing this – only Thierry will see this. So don't worry about libel."

That made me laugh.

When I began reading the first travel diary, I didn't know much about her husband except for what Gérard had told me. His name was John Mallery. He was from Boston and had gotten his law degree from Harvard. I wondered how he and Madame Mallery had met.

In the 1960s, they owned a yacht that was berthed in Antibes, near their summer home on the French Riviera. They cruised the Mediterranean for weeks at a time. They seemed partial to Italy: Portofino, Amalfi and Capri.

I was intrigued with one passage about their visit to a nightclub called the Africana on Italy's Amalfi Coast one summer's night. The club was housed in the basement of a stone tower perched at the edge of a cove. The tower had been a lookout for the dreaded Saracen pirates who ravaged the coastline in ancient times. Apparently, in the 1960s, it was a popular celebrity hangout. Madame Mallery recounts her Africana encounter that night with Vidal Sassoon, who came to their yacht the next day to style her hair.

I noted that entry with an exclamation point.

To my amazement, the Mallerys had been invited by Aristotle Onassis on a cruise to Mykonos aboard his yacht *Christina*, a nautical palace often described as a floating Xanadu, with its marble pool that transformed into a dance floor. Madame Mallery describes the yacht in detail – "the bar stools were covered with the foreskin of a minke whale."

"Seriously? Whale foreskin?" I asked at our next session. "I can't even imagine what that looks like."

"You're better off not knowing," Madame Mallery replied.

"Why would…"

"God knows." I saw a twinkle in her eyes. "Maybe it kept his libido afloat. He loved saying to his female guests – *Madame, you are sitting on the largest penis in the world.*"

She showed me a photo from that cruise of a strikingly exotic woman looking over her shoulder at the camera.

"Is that Maria Callas?" I asked.

"Yes. Those were the pre-Jackie days." Madame Mallery pursed her lips for a moment. "But even when Jackie was on the scene, Maria was never too far away."

Madame Mallery's photo albums were a Who's Who of high society on a global scale. The Mallerys dined with royalty and prime ministers and danced at the White House.

"I met Jackie when she was First Lady," Madame Mallery told me one day. "We had been invited to a private dinner with European diplomats. John was doing a lot of work in Europe then. Jackie was intrigued with his art forgery cases."

Madame Mallery was quiet for a moment. "I must admit I felt uncomfortable the first time I saw her with Ari. I couldn't imagine the Queen of Camelot keeping company with such a crass man. Ari could be very charming, but there was a vulgarity about him. Yes, he was fabulously wealthy and Jackie certainly had expensive tastes. They were perfectly matched in that way. But I couldn't imagine her going to bed with him."

I was just a toddler when Jackie married Onassis, but I remember hearing my mother, in later years, say the same thing about Jackie: "What did she ever see in *that* man?"

During the first few weeks of the project, Madame Mallery and I made good progress. We finished the travel diaries and moved on to journals she had kept when Thierry was a baby. I hoped I would meet him one day. He was a beautiful child, dressed like a 1960s version of Little Lord Fauntleroy. In one photo, he looked like a Baby Beatle, with a mod John Lennon cap and a Nehru jacket.

"We sent Thierry to English boarding school when he was 12, which was a big mistake. My husband and I had huge rows about this. Thierry was too young to be away from us, I thought. But John needed to travel more with his work and wanted me with him. He didn't want Thierry's education to suffer, so boarding school was John's solution." Madame Mallery looked at a photo of her preteen son in his school uniform. "I felt like my heart had been ripped out."

Madame Mallery gradually opened up to me as our sessions continued. She'd often reminisce as we chose the photos to be included in the book. One day, she showed me her wedding album. She and John had married in 1951 at the Mallery summer compound on Cape Cod. She was a gorgeous bride.

"My future mother-in-law had taken me to New York for a week of wedding shopping," Madame Mallery said. "I had never experienced anything like it. We found my bridal gown at the studio of an American designer who was making a big name for himself – James Galanos." She smiled. "I spent a day at Tiffany's making my wish list for our wedding-gift registry. We stayed at the Waldorf and went to fabulous dinner parties. I felt like I was marrying an American prince."

Madame Mallery never mentioned her own family. They were noticeably absent from the photo albums. I waited for her to tell me that part of her story. But she said nothing.

I could see her health was declining. She was getting thinner and weaker.

One morning in early March, I came to see her, as scheduled. I had noticed an ambulance in front of the building. Charlotte met me at the door, looking alarmed. "She is not well. They will take her to the hospital." Paramedics were in the bedroom.

Charlotte and I stepped out of Madame Mallery's line of sight, as the paramedics wheeled the stretcher to the elevator. There was no worry about her seeing us. She was barely conscious, with an oxygen mask over her face.

I went to see Madame Mallery in the hospital, but it was a brief visit. She tired easily.

She took my hand. "There's nothing more they can do," she told me. "I want you to come see me as soon as I'm discharged. This project is more urgent now."

I promised I'd come as soon as she was able.

～

Alex arrived that same week. Gérard and I met him at the airport and whisked him off to Giverny. When Gérard pulled into the moulin's courtyard, Alex whistled under his breath. "My god," he said.

As we walked to the front door, Alex looked up at the tower. "How many nights were you here alone?" he asked me.

"Three," I said. "I was *very* brave, if I do say so."

Gérard chuckled as he took my hand. "I thought about offering to stay here with you. Down the hall, of course. But I wondered if you'd suspect an ulterior motive."

"Nice guys don't always finish last," Alex said to him. "Good to know."

I wondered how things were going with Carolyn. A few weeks earlier, Alex mentioned that divorce proceedings had begun.

We had a wonderful time with Alex that week. He loved Giverny. Monet's gardens hadn't opened yet for the tourist season. But Gérard was friendly with the head gardener who gave us a private tour. The flowerbeds were showing the first growth of spring. It was the visual equivalent of hearing the first notes of the prelude to a symphony, hinting at the grand opus that was to come.

It was my first visit to the gardens with Gérard. On our tour that day, he regaled us with stories of how he and his pals had played in the gardens when they were children. "This was our stomping ground," he said. "We used to fish in the pond. The Japanese bridge was our ship. We'd fly flags from it, pretending we were pirates."

During Gérard's childhood, the house and gardens had fallen into severe neglect. In 1966, after the death of Monet's younger son Michel – who had inherited the estate from his father – the property was given to the Académie des Beaux-Arts, which began restoration work of the house and gardens in the mid-1970s. Heading the project was French art curator Gerald van der Kemp, who had led the massive restoration of the Louis XIV's palace at Versailles. He and his American wife Florence raised the funds for the Monet project mostly from Americans, including philanthropists Lila Acheson Wallace and Walter Annenberg. It was Annenberg who paid for the tunnel to the water garden. Monet's refurbished house and gardens opened to the public in 1980.

One night during Alex's stay, Gérard and I treated him to dinner at the Hôtel Baudy. I remembered my first dinner there with Gérard, not quite six months earlier. What a gift Alex had been to Gérard and me. As if reading my mind, Gérard made an emotional toast to Alex that evening: "To you, my good man." Gérard put his arm around me. "Thank you, Alex, for not letting me lose the love of my life."

Alex replied, "You've both made me a very happy guy."

During Alex's visit, we took rides through the country-side that Gérard knew so well. He took us to lovely villages, off the beaten path. One day, we had a picnic lunch on a hillside overlooking a pastoral scene the Impressionists would have painted. Below us, next to the road, was an ancient stone cross, marking the way for soldiers of the French Crusades.

While Gérard was running an errand in Vernon one afternoon, Alex and I took a walk along the Ru. When we returned to the moulin, we sat on the little bridge. It was our first time alone together since he had arrived.

"How are you doing, sweetie?" he asked, as we dangled our feet above the stream. "You've had a rough few months."

"I'm much, much better. Gérard and I are good – really good. We've been through a lot, but we're happier than ever. We have you to thank for that. Truly, Alex."

Alex smiled. "I feel I'm the lucky one in a way. I've witnessed the birth of a great love."

"How are things with you and Carolyn?"

"The marriage has been buried. We're just throwing dirt on the coffin. Mounds of dirt."

"I'm so sorry, Alex."

"It's all up to the attorneys now. The meter is running wildly. But hopefully, this will be over soon."

Alex was quiet for a moment. "How are you and the phantom doing?"

I smiled. "I feel his presence a lot. We're sitting on the bridge where he painted Marie."

"Here?"

"I'm sitting exactly where she sat."

"Do you feel her presence, too?"

"Absolutely."

"Like right now?"

I nodded. "In a good way. I try to see this as a form of enhanced perception."

"Enhanced perception." Alex looked at me. "I like that."

"When I'm here at the moulin, I feel like I've stepped into a beam of light that's meant for me. If I have a past-life connection here, so be it. What I'm experiencing in this life, right now, is extraordinary."

"Oh, Katie. I'm so happy to hear this."

I grinned at him. "I'm good with this."

"So what have you learned about this phantom – Mr. Robinson?"

"Well…he was born in Vermont, but his family moved to Evansville, Wisconsin, when he was a boy."

"Wisconsin? He was a Cheesehead? Good god, Kate. Was he a Packers fan?"

I gave Alex a withering look.

He laughed. "Sorry. Just trying to maintain some standards here."

"He had formal art training. He studied at the Chicago Academy of Design…"

"Glad to hear that."

"And at the National Academy of Design in New York. When he was 23, he went to study in Paris. The next year, in 1877, he had a painting exhibited at the Paris Salon."

"Hmm. Impressive."

"That summer, he traveled to an area near the Fontainebleau forest in France, not far from Barbizon, where landscape artists like Corot and Millet had pioneered painting from nature in the open air, in the early 19th century. While Robinson was there, he joined a colony of English-speaking artists and writers, including Robert Louis Stevenson. Incredible, isn't it? So many young artists drinking from the same cup, in a way. It was the same with Monet. When he was a student in Paris, his close friends were Cézanne, Pissarro, Sisley. His flat mate was Renoir."

"When did Robinson meet Marie?"

"The curator at the Terra Foundation says it was in 1884. He first painted her in Paris. Apparently, she was a professional model who posed for other artists at that time, including Degas."

"The curator told you about their love child?"

I nodded. "She said there was gossip in Giverny about a little girl who used to come with Marie to Giverny. Marie said the child was her niece. But a female guest at the Baudy wrote in a letter that the girl looked Robinson."

"The painting of the little girl with the cherries – when did he paint that?"

"1891. The girl looks about three or four in the painting. Robinson didn't start coming to Giverny until 1887. It's possible Marie gave birth to her before his days in Giverny. But there's no documentation that the girl with the cherries is the love child."

"And when was Robinson's last visit here?"

"1892. He sailed back to New York from Le Havre, in December. According to his diary, he went to Paris a few days before he left, to see Marie."

I felt so sad in that moment, sitting where she had sat, with my hand on the rusted railing. "He never saw her again."

"When did he die?"

"Four years later. In 1896."

"How could he leave her behind – with a child?"

"I've wondered about that, too. Sonia, the curator, says they had agreed not to marry and she suspects it was due to his frail health. He was not well off financially. He taught at art schools during the winter months. Apparently, he intended to return to Giverny – according to his letters to Monet."

"How did he die?"

"A severe asthma attack. He was just 43."

"Ach. Such a sad story." Alex patted my arm. "I wonder what happened to Marie. Did they write to each other during those four years?"

"Most likely. Sonia says those letters have never been found."

～

That was Alex's last day with us in Giverny, at least for that visit. I felt invigorated by his company and at peace with myself. I had accepted my *enhanced perception* of past lives at the moulin as a strange gift. Underlying everything was the profound love I felt for Gérard and knowing that he loved me as deeply in return. Even with the loss of our baby, which we would silently grieve for some time, we were strongly linked arm-in-arm with each other.

Days were coming when I'd be so grateful for that – and for Alex's unfailing friendship.

12

Madame Mallery called me the day after she was discharged from the hospital. It was the middle of March.

When I arrived at her apartment the next morning, Charlotte didn't escort me to the sitting room. Instead, she led me upstairs to a grand bedroom that made the bed look like a piece of dollhouse furniture. The room was decorated in pink and green. The walls were covered with seafoam green brocade. Pink satin curtains, trimmed with mint green tassels, dressed the oversized windows that looked onto a landscaped back courtyard. An immense floral rug, in pastel shades, covered much of the parquet floor.

I couldn't help but notice a large Renoir nude on the wall opposite the bed. I wondered if it was a giclée copy of the original.

Madame Mallery answered my unspoken question: "It's the real thing."

She was sitting in bed bolstered by lovely satin pillows. She wore an elegant powder-pink peignoir set. I had found a peignoir set my mother had worn on her honeymoon, in her cedar chest after she died. It was comforting to see such old-fashioned elegance still existed. Madame Mallery's peignoirs, Charlotte later told me, were originals by Coco Chanel.

Madame Mallery looked gaunt and frail. She motioned for me to sit on an upholstered chair beside the bed. That simple gesture seemed to be an effort. "I hope you'll be comfortable here. I'm sorry I have to do this from my bed. I don't have my legs back yet."

Charlotte brought our usual tea-and-coffee tray. But Madame Mallery had no appetite. She wanted to begin work immediately.

"I suppose you've wondered – the professional journalist that you are – why I've not mentioned anything about my childhood family." She waited for me to respond.

"Yes, I've noticed their absence in your journals and photos."

"This is not an easy story for me to tell. I wish I had done it sooner. I don't know if I have the strength for it now. But I must tell it. Thierry needs to know it."

"You've not told him?"

"Never."

I had brought a tape recorder with me that day. I had never recorded our sessions. But I wondered if she'd like me to do this now, especially if she was recounting stories that she wanted me to write verbatim.

She balked at the idea at first. "I've never spoken a word of this story. Not even to John."

I was stunned to hear that.

"You will be the first person I've told this story to. Ever. Now do you understand the reason for the contract?" She looked at me intently. Her blue eyes were glassy, but they still held a spark of her tenacity.

Part of me wanted to leave the room. I hadn't expected this burden. I nodded. "Would you like me to record this?" I asked her again.

"Yes," she said quietly.

I took a deep breath and turned on the recorder. I pulled a pad from my bag to take notes as she spoke.

What transpired in the next half hour was like a death-bed confession. She had obviously thought about how she would tell this story to me. She didn't struggle for words. There was little emotion in her voice, until she got to the end.

She began with the story of her mother, who had been a seamstress in Paris in the 1920s and 30s. She worked for a tailor whose shop was near the boarding house where they lived in Montparnasse. Madame Mallery never knew her father. "I was conceived out of wedlock," she told me matter-of-factly. "My mother was 38 when she had me. Alone, with the meager income of a seamstress."

Madame Mallery was 13 when the Nazis invaded Paris in 1940. "It was a murderous time, when you had to watch your back and be careful who you counted as your friends. My mother was sympathetic with the Resistance. Some-times, I'd see odd scraps of fabric she'd bring home from the shop. She said she had more mending to do that she couldn't finish during the day. But this wasn't the work she was getting paid to do. She was sewing clothes for soldiers of the night."

Madame Mallery's hand shook as she took a sip of her tea. The china cup rattled as she set it back on the saucer.

"My mother was having an affair with an SS officer, to get black-market items for the two us to survive. One night, a Frenchman I had never seen before came to the boarding house. He warned my mother she was in danger and begged her to come away with him. They had a heated argument. He told her he would come back in an hour, for both of us."

Madame Mallery paused for moment. She looked out window and then back at me. "Twenty minutes later, three SS officers – including her *lover* – stormed the house, looking for her. She and I hid in the closet. There was nowhere else for us to hide. They found her easily. But they didn't see me. I was a scrawny little waif then.

"They threw her on the bed. I could hear them raping her. They were savages. She pleaded, begging them to stop. When they finished with her, her lover pulled out his pistol and held it to her forehead – taunting her, spitting in her face. And then he pulled the trigger."

I couldn't bear to hear another word. But Madame Mallery continued, as she laid her head back on the pillows.

"I stayed in the closet all night. The SS surrounded the house, waiting for the Frenchman to return. No one came. In the morning, someone took away my mother's body. I don't know who. I didn't make a sound. I stayed in the closet for two days. The landlady, who lived downstairs, came to clear out the room and found me, dazed and incoherent. She fed me and got me on my feet. A few days later, she took me to a convent in another part of Paris. The nuns saved me." She fingered the gold cross at her throat. "I'm a very religious woman to this day."

Madame Mallery closed her eyes. I sat quietly, wondering if I should turn off the recorder.

Eyes still closed, she whispered, "I've kept this a secret until now. I feel a weight has been lifted from me."

I didn't know if I dared asked what happened next. But there was a missing chunk of this story. "Madame Mallery, did you stay at the convent for the remainder of the war?"

"Yes. The nuns had taken in a number of orphans. They cared for me and saw to my education. I considered becoming one of them." She looked sheepishly at me. "But I wasn't a nun at heart."

She looked around her lavishly decorated bedroom. "I wanted this." She gazed at the Renoir painting and smiled. "I wanted to marry well and have a life my mother couldn't imagine. I never looked back on the darkness of my childhood. I was 17 when the war in Europe ended. The first years after the war were difficult for everyone. But that worked to my advantage. It leveled the playing field, which made it easier for someone like me to get a footing."

"How did you meet your husband?"

"He was an army officer stationed in Paris during the Occupation. We met at a club in Montmartre. I swept him off his feet, he always said. For me, he was a prince from a fairy tale."

"What did you tell him about your past?"

"That my parents died during the war and that I ended up in a convent orphanage. Not a lie, really. Except for the part about my father. I never knew what happened to him. I was so ashamed that I was illegitimate."

She looked at me, trying to read my face. "Are you shocked?"

"Yes."

She smiled. "I appreciate candor."

"Not because I think your story is scandalous or shameful. I'm shocked at the tragedy you've known – and amazed how you've risen above it."

"That's the secret of having a life worth living."

~

As Charlotte escorted me to the door that day, Madame Mallery called to her from the bedroom.

When she returned, Charlotte said to me in French, "Madame would like you to leave the tape. You can transcribe it later."

I popped the tape out of the recorder. Madame Mallery hadn't lost her vise-grip.

When I got back to my apartment, Gérard was making lunch. He took one look at me and asked, "What happened to you?"

"My god." I plopped myself down at the kitchen table. "If I tell you, I'll have to kill you. You know the rules."

"That bad?"

I shook my head in disbelief. "Didn't you once say to me you couldn't imagine she had skeletons in her closet?"

"Words to that effect."

I put my head down on the table.

He pulled up a chair, as if expecting me to spill the juicy beans.

I looked up at him. "You *know* I can't tell you."

He smiled devilishly. "After lunch, let's take a nap. Pretend you're sleeping and tell me everything."

"No pillow talk, remember?"

"The contract doesn't say anything about talking in your sleep."

~

Madame Mallery had asked me to come back the next day. I expected Charlotte would lead me to the sitting room, where I would be transcribing the big confession.

But when Charlotte met me at the door that morning, she said, "Madame would like to see you upstairs."

Madame Mallery looked remarkably better, as if, indeed, a weight had lifted from her.

"Good morning," she said. She was in bed, wearing another stunning peignoir set. I noticed a small stack of yellowed letters, tied with pink ribbon, on the bed next to her.

"Good morning, Madame Mallery."

"So you've come back for another day of startling revelations?"

I smiled at her. I couldn't imagine she had any more secrets up her billowing chiffon sleeves.

Charlotte brought our tea and coffee, as usual. I had come to look forward to the pastry treats on that tray.

"You will want to record today's session as well," Madame Mallery said, as Charlotte poured her tea. The tape sat on Madame Mallery's night table.

Madame Mallery never spoke of personal matters in front of Charlotte. She wasn't friendly with Charlotte. Madame Mallery ruled her staff. She wasn't abusive, but she maintained aloofness and could be callously dismissive.

That day, Madame Mallery was impatient with both Charlotte and me. "Charlotte, leave us now," she said curtly.

I was about to take a bite of the pastry du jour, when Madame Mallery looked at me with exasperation. "Miss Morgan, *that* can wait."

She waited for Charlotte to close the bedroom door, as I put the divine-looking *chouquette* back on the plate.

"I have some old letters I would like you to transcribe," she said. "They must stay here at the apartment. There are 17 of them in all. I will count them every day before you leave."

My blood began roiling. "Why is it that you don't trust me?" I asked her. I knew she was a sick woman, but I wasn't going to excuse her imbedded bad behavior. "I have no desire to take anything of yours. In fact, I'd much rather leave it *all* here with you."

"We're too far into this to start quarreling now," she said, untying the ribbon around the letters. She handed me the top one from the stack. "Please quiet yourself and read this."

I inhaled and said a little prayer for patience.

I carefully unfolded the letter. It was dated January 1887 and began with *Mon cher*...

The penmanship was very feminine, with lots of curves and swooping tails. The stationery was elegant and finely textured. The edges of the paper had aged, but the ink was only slightly faded.

The woman wrote, in French, about the bad weather in Paris and how cold Degas' studio was on wintery days. "I told him I will not remove a single article of clothing – not even my scarf – until he buys more wood for the stove." And then she adds, "But of course you know, my darling, no man has ever seen my naked body but you."

The letter goes on with news from Paris. The woman knows a number of the young painters of the day – Georges Seurat, Henri de Toulouse-Lautrec, Vincent van Gogh.

She closes with hopes that he is well and that she will hear again from him soon.

The letter is signed: M.

I sensed Madame Mallery was gauging my reaction, but I didn't look at her. She held out the next letter on the stack for me to take.

I laid the first letter on the bed and took the second. It appeared to have been written on a sheet of sketch paper.

I glanced at the date – March 1889 – and then looked at the scratchy signature: Theo.

Madame Mallery was in possession of the missing letters.

"Where did you get these?" I asked her incredulously.

"They belonged to my mother," she said.

"Your mother. How did she get them?"

"From her mother."

It took a minute for it all to sink in. "Her mother was Marie?"

Madame Mallery nodded.

"And your mother was…"

Madame Mallery smiled. "The scandalous love child."

13

It broke my heart to think of the little girl in the soiled blue dress, with cherry juice on her cheeks, as the woman who died in her bed with a Nazi bullet to her brain.

I kept telling myself that I had concocted the story of the little girl as the love child. I had no proof that she was Theodore and Marie's daughter. But deep in my heart, somewhere in my cellular memory, I didn't think I was wrong about this.

For the next several days, as I read Theo and Marie's letters, I pieced together their love affair. But as I suspected, it wasn't always a rosy story. Sadness stalked them like a shadow they couldn't shake.

Their relationship was intensely sexual. I could read that between the lines. I felt myself being drawn into their affair. As I'd walk through the streets of Paris, I'd imagine them in an artist's atelier, making love. I'd lie awake some nights, with Gérard sound asleep beside me, imagining myself as Marie giving herself to Theo. I could feel his lips on mine, the roughness of his moustache. One night, I imagined him penetrating me. I could feel the hardness of him inside me. I was alone at my apartment that night. I was so aroused, I made myself come, just to relieve the throbbing pain of desire. Theo was real to me that night. I fell asleep, sublimely happy. But when I awoke, I felt like I had betrayed Gérard.

I felt strangely pregnant with this secret story, in a wonderful way at first. But as the days wore on, during the tedium of transcribing the letters, I knew it was beginning to gnaw at me.

There had been jealousy in their relationship. In one exchange of letters, Marie questioned Theo's love for her and suspected a girl in the village of trying to seduce him. I immediately thought of the "wench in the grass," as Alex called her – the girl in the floppy hat who had coyly smiled at Theo as he photographed her. Marie asked Theo accusingly if he had invited this attention – and more to the point, had he slept with her?

Theo vehemently denied he had strayed and assured Marie that she was the only woman he could ever love. What surprised me was that he seemed to be trying to find a way for them to marry. He wrote of his hopes of selling his paintings at an exhibition in the U.S. that winter, allowing him to return to Paris with enough funds to support them. He asked about "A," saying how much he missed her.

I went to Giverny for Easter weekend, in late March. On that Saturday afternoon, Gérard was doing some finishing work in the gatehouse. I decided to take a nap in the fairy-tale bed. I would be sorry when the tourists began arriving in May, when Gérard re-opened for the season. I had become very possessive of *my* bed.

As I lay on that bed, I imagined Theo and Marie in this room, as I had many times before. Except in this daydream, I became Marie. I saw myself unbuttoning the ruffled striped dress. It fell to the floor as Theo quickly untied my corset. He pulled me to the makeshift bed on the floor. His shirt was unbuttoned, his trousers undone. He crawled on top of me, hungrily kissing me.

Suddenly, I heard the bedroom door creak as Gérard entered the room. My heart raced, like I had been caught with my panties down. My thoughts flashed to Pamela.

Gérard came to the bed, smiling at me. "There you are," he said. "I wondered where you had disappeared to."

He quickly shed his clothes and crawled into bed next to me. "Do you think we'll ever get tired of this?" he asked playfully.

"I hope not," I said.

"Me, too."

He began kissing me. I closed my eyes, letting myself continue my fantasy daydream. I was so engorged, I thought I was going to explode.

My orgasm was incredible. At the peak of it, I quietly said *Theo*, on the exhale of a moan.

It was one of those moments, when the earth seems to stop spinning for a moment.

Gérard was inside me, on the verge of his climax, but quickly his whole body went limp. He raised up on his elbows and looked at me.

"What did you just say?"

It was the question that hung in the air for the rest of the weekend. I tried to laugh it off. But collateral damage had been done.

The next day, we went to Gérard's parent's house for Easter lunch. It was a lovely spring day. We were out in the garden, which was literally springing to life.

Friends of the family were there. There were a dozen of us at a long wooden table under the budding fruit trees. Conversation turned to the old days. An elderly gentleman reminisced about his father's stories of Giverny. "An American artist used to stay here, in this house, with her mother. She was from Boston, I think. This garden appeared in her paintings. Theodore Robinson took many photographs here."

I recalled Sonia saying that she had not found the property where Mariquita Gill had stayed, where Robinson had photographed Marie for his painting *The Layette*.

I looked around, searching for a telltale sign. It only took a moment. There, by the wall at the far end of the garden, was an old gnarled fruit tree, with a branch that looked like a bent elbow – now supported with a pole.

I got up from the table, without a word, and walked to the tree. I ran my hand along its bark. I was standing at the spot where Marie had sewn her layette.

Gérard was next to me in a minute. "*Chérie*, what's wrong?"

"Nothing." I said. "I just have a little headache. Would you mind if I went back to the moulin?"

He looked concerned.

"Bring me some dessert," I said, trying to sound like myself.

I thanked his parents for a lovely lunch and excused myself. I walked backed to the moulin, a short distance, and called a cab to take me to Vernon. Before it arrived, I left a note for Gérard on the dining table.

An hour later, I was on the next train back to Paris.

~

I burst into the apartment that evening and went straight to my computer. I thanked god that Alex wasn't religious, sitting at a church service somewhere in Chicago. It was Easter morning his time.

"Katie!" he cried, when he saw me on video. "How are you? What'd you get from the Easter Bunny?"

"Alex…"

"Oh no, a Paris rat ate your chocolate rabbit," he said. When I didn't laugh, he got serious. "Kate, what's wrong?"

My story made no sense at first. But Alex is good at getting story elements in chronological order. It took him a minute to comprehend the seriousness of Madame Mallery's stranglehold on me. "Why did Gérard let you agree to this?" he asked in disbelief.

"It was *my* decision, Alex," I said defensively. I didn't want to lay the blame on Gérard. "She offered me good money, but I had no idea how horrible her secrets were."

I didn't reveal Madame Mallery's war stories – I still felt honor-bound. But I told him about Theo and Marie's missing letters.

"Alex, I'm falling back down the rabbit hole." I could hear panic rising in my voice. "I'm having dreams again. I see myself as Marie. I *am* Marie."

"Katie, calm down."

The night before I had dreamt I was having a baby. There was blood all over the bed. Theo was holding my hand. I dug my nails into his flesh as the contractions came harder. A doctor finally arrived. When he realized the baby was breach, he reached up inside me and turned her. The pain was excruciating, as he pulled a baby girl out of my womb. But within moments, I heard her healthy cries.

I had awakened from the dream, screaming. Gérard held me. But I could feel his strain and fear as he tried to comfort me.

Alex and I talked for a half hour, maybe more. He is so good at laying his calming hands on your shoulders, even from halfway around the planet.

When I told him I had called Gérard "Theo" in our naptime lovemaking the previous afternoon, Alex ran his hands through his hair and murmured, "Holy Christ."

For some reason, that made me laugh. "Very Easter-y of you, Alex."

He laughed, too. Alex and I never lost our sense of humor – no matter how dire the circumstances.

We stayed on skype another hour. It was almost 7 p.m. in Paris. Suddenly, my doorbell rang.

"My god, Alex. It's probably Gérard. What should I do?"

"Answer the door?"

"Don't go away," I begged him.

"I'm right here."

On my door-buzzer video monitor, I could see Gérard standing at the street. In a few minutes, he was knocking at my door.

"Alex!" I whispered.

"Open the door, Kate. It's okay," Alex whispered back on skype.

It wasn't okay. Not really.

Gérard stood in the doorway, looking disheveled. "What the hell is going on?"

As he stepped inside the apartment, Alex called out, "Hi Gérard! It's Alex coming to you live from Chicago."

Gérard looked at me, totally baffled. "Are we on the radio?"

Alex and I burst out laughing. Gérard started laughing, too, only because Alex and I were doubled over.

"No, my love, we're not on the radio." I hugged Gérard and gave him a peck on the cheek.

Gérard sat down at the table and pulled a bottle of wine out of his backpack. "I don't know about the two of you, but I need a glass of this."

"Me, too," I said.

Gérard gave me a serious look. "Especially you."

The three of us talked for another hour. Alex so eloquently explained to us both his theory about what happens when cellular memory wakes up from amnesia.

"There is no hard science behind this, but I think what Kate has been experiencing is an extraordinary spiritual phenomenon. Katie, you are a highly evolved, intelligent human being and have been presented with an amazing opportunity to delve into the far reaches of your soul and psyche. But if this is freaking you out, shut down this whole business with Madame Mallery. Rip up the contract and tell her you're done."

Gérard nodded. "I'm with you, Alex."

Alex looked at me. "What do you think, Kate?"

"I'm done." I felt so relieved to say that.

14

The next morning, I called Madame Mallery and told her I needed to see her immediately. I didn't tell her Gérard would be coming with me.

When we got off the elevator at her apartment, the guard wasn't there. It was Easter Monday. Maybe Madame Mallery benevolently had given him the day off.

Charlotte answered the door and looked surprised to see Gérard. "It's okay," I said to her.

"May I give Madame Mallery your name?" she asked Gérard.

At that moment, Madame Mallery appeared in the doorway of the sitting room. She was elegantly dressed, a Hermès scarf around her head.

"Gérard," she said, smiling. I wondered if she had been expecting him.

She was charming and coquettish, as sweet as a kitten.

Gérard didn't waste time getting to the reason for our visit. He handed her a fat envelope.

"Gérard, what's this?"

"The money you've given Kate. Count it, if you'd like. I think it's all there."

"You offend me, Gérard."

"No, no, Margot. You're not going to turn this on us. Kate came here, in good faith, to help you with your *gift* to Thierry. But what has happened here in these past few weeks was way more than she bargained for."

I took the contract out of my handbag and tore it in half. "I will never publicize your secrets, Madame Mallery. But I'm finished."

And then Madame Mallery did something that surprised us both. She apologized.

"I am so sorry, Miss Morgan, for laying my burden on you. I'm a dying woman who needs absolution. I sincerely apologize for any trauma this has caused you."

Madame Mallery sadly looked at Gérard. "I adore you like a son, Gérard. Please forgive me."

Gérard embraced her. My heart melted as she wept on his shoulder. In the perversion of my past-life time traveling, I felt very maternal toward her in that moment.

∿

That morning, Charlotte served the three of us tea and coffee. Madame Mallery openly discussed with Gérard the story she had shared with me – not the excruciating details of her mother's death, but her very humble life as a child.

"My mother's name was Anjou. If I'd had a daughter, I would have named her that," she told us.

"Did she ever speak to you about your grandmother?" I asked.

"Yes, she told me Marie had married a man who ran an art studio in Paris. He died during the First World War. Marie died in 1921, during the great influenza epidemic. She was 59. I never knew her." Madame Mallery folded the corner of the linen napkin on her lap. "My mother had a tragic life. She raised me alone and tried to provide for me in the best way she could during horrendously difficult times." She straightened herself as she spoke. "But I was determined my life would be *nothing* like hers."

I could see her energy was failing. "I think Gérard and I should go," I said to her.

Madame Mallery handed me the envelope. "This is yours, my dear. Think of it as hazard pay."

I looked at Gérard. He smiled and nodded. "Thank you, Madame Mallery," I said.

"I'm going to Giverny tomorrow," she told us. "Will you be there this week? I'd like you both to come to the house. I have something I'd like to show you."

"We're heading back there today, in fact," Gérard said.

"Good. Call me on Wednesday, Kate, and we'll set a day to meet."

It was the first time Madame Mallery had ever called me Kate.

∼

That Friday, Gérard and I took a drive to *Les Marguerites*.

The house appeared even more immense in the daylight. We drove under the chestnut trees that shaded the driveway and came around the curve to see a stunning view of the house. Around the fountain in the front circle of the driveway, wild daisies were in their spring glory.

Another car was parked in the driveway, along with a FedEx truck.

Pierre Gaston greeted us as we entered the foyer. "You're just in time."

Gérard and I didn't know what we were in time for, but we gamely followed him into the drawing room.

Madame Mallery waved to us from her regal-looking chair that perhaps Josephine Bonaparte had sat upon to change her silk stockings in days gone by.

"Come, darlings," Madame Mallery called cheerfully to us. "Have a seat. The unpacking is about to begin."

Two FedEx couriers, wielding crowbars, were pulling huge staples out of a large wooden crate. It was a delicate operation despite the brute strength it required.

Madame Mallery was like a child on Christmas morning.

"Is this a new acquisition for the museum?" Gérard asked.

She wagged her finger at him. "No, no. This is *my* baby."

"A new or old baby?" he asked.

"You will see, you will see." She could hardly contain her excitement.

The uncrating process took about 20 minutes. I had never seen how paintings are packed for shipping. The couriers, who were clearly specialists in this type of delivery, carefully disassembled the crate and slowly began removing the layers of padding and wrapping. When they finally got down to the last layer, they put on protective gloves. Madame Mallery instructed us all to close our eyes.

"No peeking," she insisted. "I want to be the first to lay eyes on her."

I could hear the couriers remove the final layer of wrapping. Madame Mallery let out a little gasp. At first, I thought the painting had been damaged.

But then she said, "She's as lovely as ever."

"Now?" Gérard asked.

"Yes, now," she said.

There in front of us, balanced by the gloved hands of the FedEx couriers, was the little girl with the cherries – our darling marauder.

"She has been gone for a long time," Madame Mallery said. "I'm so glad she's finally home."

Gérard smiled and reached for my hand. "We saw her in Chicago."

Madame Mallery looked surprised for a moment. "You both were in Chicago?"

We nodded.

"It was my favorite painting of the exhibition," I said. "I asked the curator about its owner."

"She was sworn to secrecy," Pierre Gaston informed me.

"She kept her word," I assured him.

Madame Mallery looked at me. "Aren't you going to ask, good journalist that you are?"

"I think I already know the answer," I said.

Madame Mallery held a theatrical beat, for effect, and then said, "This is my mother."

~~◦

Madame Mallery died a few weeks later at *Les Margue-rites*. She called me to her bedside a few days before she passed away. She wanted to go over the final details of the book. She had asked me to oversee its production. I had already met with the printer in Paris.

"I had hoped to see the proof copy," she told me. She was hanging on by a thread. She and I both knew the end was near.

"I will take care of everything," I promised her. "Have you told Thierry about the book?"

"No. He knows nothing about it – or my sordid past."

"Madame Mallery – don't you think he'd want to hear you tell him this story?"

"I don't have the strength for that, Kate. Not now."

I kissed her on the cheek before I said good-bye that day.

A Marauder hung beside Madame Mallery's bed. I said good-bye to her as well.

As I walked down the grand staircase at *Les Marguerites*, I remembered Madame Mallery standing, larger than life, on those steps the first time I was drawn to the bright light of her flame.

After that day, I never saw her again.

15

A few weeks later, several hundred people attended a memorial service for Madame Mallery in the garden at the American Impressionist museum in Giverny. It was a beautiful April day. A portrait of her by fashion photographer Richard Avedon was on display, next to *A Marauder*. I hadn't expected to see my little girl again.

I laid a bouquet, tied with ribbon, on the pile of bouquets others had brought in Madame Mallery's memory. Many of the bouquets were laced with daisies. Margot was Madam Mallery's nickname: Her given name was Marguerite – the French word for daisy. I had made my bouquet for her from the blossoms of a tree behind the moulin. A cherry tree.

I caught a glimpse of Thierry that day. Gérard pointed him out to me. I hoped I'd have another opportunity to speak with him privately. He was surrounded by his mother's friends, museum colleagues and admirers who were expressing their condolences and sharing their memories of her.

The next day, I returned to the moulin after a run to a grocery store in Vernon. A sleek Mercedes sports coupe was in the courtyard.

Gérard was out on the terrace with Thierry.

"I'm delighted to meet you, Kate." Thierry clasped my hands between his. He had a beautiful smile. "My mother told me so much about you."

"Really?"

"On the night she died, we had a nice long talk." He smiled. "As was her style, she did most of the talking. She was amazingly lucid." Thierry held my hands tight and then said, "She told me everything. She said she had told you the story as well."

"Yes. And quite a story it is."

Gérard and I sat with Thierry for a while.

"I don't know why she kept these secrets from me all these years," he said. "I'm sorry for her tragic childhood. I wish I had known all that she had endured. Maybe I would have been a better-behaved teenager." He smiled at Gérard.

"No way," Gérard teased him.

Thierry laughed. "But I'm very happy to be the great-grandson of an American painter and his beautiful lover. She was a stunner."

Gérard smiled at me.

"It solves another mystery that I've wondered about all my life," Thierry said.

"What's that?" I asked.

"My middle name – Théodore – I've never been able to explain it until now. I'd like you to use my full name in the book: Thierry Théodore Mallery."

"Are we printing just one copy?" I asked him.

"Seems a bit extravagant, doesn't it?"

"It was her wish," I said.

"God help us both if we don't honor it." He laughed. "Before I forget, I have something for you." He removed a small square envelope from his jacket pocket. My mother asked me to give this to you on the night she died. It's a gift from her to you. She said you would know its significance."

"A woman of intrigue – even now. Thank you, Thierry."

"I best be going. Next time you're both in Paris, I'd like to take you to dinner. We can celebrate my new identity." He shook Gérard's hand. "Good to see you, old friend."

"Same, Thierry. Again, I'm so sorry about your mother. She was a great woman. *Une femme formidable.*"

"She was indeed." Thierry turned to me and kissed me on both cheeks. "Thank you, Kate. She confessed she put you through the wringer. She didn't mean to unburden herself on you."

"I know. No lasting harm."

Gérard and I walked Thierry to the courtyard and waved good-bye as he drove away.

Standing behind me, Gérard slipped his arms around my waist. It felt good to lean against him. "How are you?" he asked.

"Tired." It was a hot day.

"Why don't you go upstairs and lie down? I'll come join you shortly. How does that sound?"

"Sounds wonderful."

~

I went up to the room and opened the windows. I looked down at the foamy water splashing from the paddle wheel. The stream was a clear emerald green. I imagined its coolness and the silky feel of the submerged bed of moss by the bridge.

I unbuttoned my blouse and tossed it on a chair. I stood at the bathroom sink, splashing water on my face and neck, letting the water soak my bra. I patted myself dry with a fluffy towel, took off my skirt and lay down on the bed.

I looked up at the vault of the ceiling and listened to the water cascading below me. I felt Theo's presence in the room that day. Mostly, I felt his love.

I opened the envelope from Madame Mallery. Inside was an old photograph and a note from her.

> *The question I have for you, dear Kate: Do you know more about Marie than you're letting on? I think so.*
> *I give you this photo Theo took of her and "our" little girl.*
> *With much love and gratitude ~ Margot*

The photo was faded and creased. It's of Marie, holding the hand of little Anjou, who looks much like Theo's rendering of her. Behind them is the gate from the painting. Anjou is holding a clump of cherries.

I closed my eyes and saw myself walking though a cherry orchard toward a tall, lanky man. I feel Anjou's sticky hand in mine. Theo picks her up. "You're a little marauder," he tells her. She carefully places a cherry in his mouth. "Mmmm. So good," he says. "Almost as sweet as you." He kisses her cheek. Theo puts his arm around me, holding me close. Anjou feeds me a cherry, too.

My face was wet with tears. I opened my eyes to see Gérard standing by the bed.

"What is it, *chérie*?" he asked tenderly.

He sat down on the bed beside me and looked at the photo. "Marie?" he asked.

I nodded. "And Anjou."

He put the photo on the night table. "You belong in *this* world," he said to me. "I'm the one who loves you."

Gérard kissed me gently and wiped away my tears.

∼

We conceived a much-wanted child that afternoon in the fairy-tale bed. A little girl, with cherry-blonde hair, as we liked to describe it. We baptized her at the little church in Giverny, next to where Monet is buried, and afterward, had a celebration lunch at the Hôtel Baudy. Gérard and I stole a little time that afternoon to take a stroll through the Baudy's back garden. I happily imagined the beautiful days Theo and Marie had spent there, with their little girl running along the garden paths.

Our baby's godfather carried her in his arms most of that afternoon at the Baudy, showing her off to everyone, including the college clan from Chicago. Naturally, our daughter's godfather would be Alex and, of course, her name would be Marie.

~

It all happened so long ago – my first visit to Gérard's moulin. My happiness since has blurred the years like the vapory air blurs the landscape of mystical Giverny. It was my destiny to return there – to re-visit another lifetime – in order to embrace what was waiting for me in this one. Finding Gérard was a gift from Theo – who released me from my heartache, my longing for lost love…and my secret. But the memory of Theo in a shower of cherry blossoms, with his arms around me and our beloved little girl, will live in my heart forever.

~ fini ~

AUTHOR'S EPILOGUE

The story of *The Secret of Marie* began in Giverny, in the fall of 2004. I had gone to this idyllic village in the Seine valley to write an article about an art school run by American artist Gale Bennett and his wife, Cello.

I stayed at the moulin and was the only guest there during most of my visit. I'll never forget the first night – checking each room to be sure I was really alone. And when I reached the top floor of the moulin's tower and opened the last door, to what I thought would be a bathroom…

Is this sounding familiar?

Like Kate, I felt a rush of cold air and hurried back to my room – with its fairy-tale bed – and tried to gather my courage. I sang to my phantom that night and every night. The *chouette* sang, too.

It was during that visit to Giverny that I first learned of Theodore Robinson. I lingered at his paintings at the Impressionist museum in Giverny – then called Musée d'Art Américain Giverny – and at the locations where he had painted. One of his favorite settings was the moulin and its little bridge. I was especially drawn to his paintings of Marie.

Three years later, in 2007, I went to an exhibition at the San Diego Museum of Art called *Impressionist Giverny: A Colony of Artists, 1885-1915*, conceived and created by the Musée d'Art Américain Giverny/Terra Foundation for American Art. It was there that I saw *A Marauder* for the first time. I was captivated by that darling little girl, holding the clump of cherries. I stood there for several minutes, wondering who she was. And then I heard a man whisper over my shoulder: *You're here.*

Like Kate, I turned around to see who was standing behind me. But there was no one.

My journey down the rabbit hole began that day.

It didn't consume me, but my soulful connection to Theodore Robinson greatly intrigued me. As a writer with a vivid imagination, I love stories that involve time shifts and parallel universes. I'm fascinated with the concept of déjà vu and the possibility of past-life encounters in the present.

During my first visit to the moulin in 2004, I heard a story that Robinson may have used *my* room as a studio. Whether that's true or not, I felt his lovely presence there. When I later learned about his love affair with Marie, I imagined what might have transpired in that room, perched above the moulin's paddle wheel.

Over the years, I've fallen asleep many nights in that room at the moulin, listening to the rushing water of the Ru. The sound of it fills my dreams that take me back in time. When I'm at the moulin, extraordinary things happen to me. I feel dreamy and inspired, like I've stepped into a beam of light that's meant for me.

One spring evening at the Hôtel Baudy, I met an American man, who was also traveling alone. He was sitting at a table on the Baudy's terrace under the linden trees when I arrived. My favorite waitress thought it would be a good idea if we had dinner together. He was game and so was I. Harold was a delightful dinner partner – a blues musician who had spent his career as a clinical psychologist and had written a thesis about the correlation between humor, creativity and self-esteem. As fate would have it, he was staying at the moulin. Before he left the next morning, he played for me on the out-of-tune piano in the moulin's sitting room – pop standards and love songs, some of them his own. The spirit of his beautiful music transcended those tinny keys.

As he drove away that day, I stood at the little bridge and felt the love of Theo and Marie. More than once, I've sat at the spot by the bridge where she posed for *La Débâcle*. I've held the rusted railing and gazed at the field she would have seen as she posed for Theo there.

That's the beauty of Giverny. Much of it hasn't changed since the days of Monet and the American painters who followed him to this enchanting hamlet in the Normandy countryside more than a century ago.

As I constructed this story, I tried to stay true to the historical facts. When I read historical fiction, I always appreciate when the author reveals the line between the story's history and fabrication: The modern-day layer of this story is fiction. But it is rooted in my ethereal connection to Robinson.

Marie remains an art-history mystery. Not even her last name is known. She seemed to vanish into the ether after Robinson's last visit to Giverny in 1892. The story Madame Mallery tells of Marie's later life is fiction. The story of Anjou (I named her after a lovely young girl I know) is also fiction. Madame Mallery is invented, too. The content of the letters between Theodore and Marie is fiction. It seems those letters have disappeared into the ether as well.

The gossip about Theodore and Marie's love child was documented in two letters, written to Boston painter Philip Leslie Hale in 1890, by a woman staying at the Hôtel Baudy. There is no documentation that the little girl in *A Marauder* is the love child. I imagined her as Theodore and Marie's daughter when I first saw her at the San Diego Museum of Art in 2007.

My dinner partner Harold gave Alex his delightful sense of humor. Alex's explanations of "cellular memory" and past-life encounters come from my dear friend Marty, who has a highly evolved soul and great wisdom about the ways of the universe.

Gérard comes from the wistful yearnings of my heart. I fell in love with Gérard the day I started writing the first draft. In the outline, I drew him as a minor character. But when he walked into the dining room, splattered with yellow paint, on Kate's first morning at the moulin, he looked at me – as if he were an actor on a stage for an audition – and said to me, *I'm NOT a minor character*. He was so right. That's the joy of writing for me. I'm initially the story's creator. But in the end, I'm just the facilitator. Before too long, the characters take over and all I have to do is take dictation.

Except for our shared love of Theodore, Kate are I are not so much alike. I let her soul take wing that day at the beach, early in the book, when she does a pathetic cartwheel that set in motion her plan to move to Paris. (I did pathetic cartwheels as a kid, but haven't attempted one in decades.)

Kate and I do have some similarities on our résumés. We both went to Northwestern University, though I graduated a decade before she did. She majored in art history; I graduated with a master's degree from the Medill School of Journalism. We both suffered frozen-eyeball syndrome, standing on a Chicago L platform in winter. She returned to southern California, her home state, after graduation. I spent my tween and teenage years living in the Chicago suburbs and loved going to the Art Institute. In my 20s, I worked as a journalist in Washington, D.C. and New York, before I eventually settled in southern California. I've called Pasadena my home since 1987. My second home is Florence, Italy, where I landed after my only child went off to college. Like Kate, I was ready for an adventure and like many writers before me, found a muse in Florence, where I wrote my two previous books – a memoir called *Tales from Tavanti: An American Woman's Mid-Life Adventure in Italy* and a novel (or not) called *Not a True Story*. Early in my journalism career, I worked as a writer/columnist for *People* magazine, in New York and Los Angeles, and in that job, was a guest on *The Oprah Winfrey Show*.

I dedicate *The Secret of Marie* to the lovely people of Giverny who assisted with my research; fed me well; gave me a fairy-tale bed in a room called Chambre Marguerite (*merci*, Stephanie and Gérard); and invited me to participate in a *plein-air* painting class (thank you, Caroline and Rich) that helped me appreciate the experience of the artists who are part of Giverny's legacy.

I've spent countless hours at Monet's gardens in Giverny, mesmerized by this floral heaven on earth. I applaud the Claude Monet Foundation and the team of gardeners, led by renowned English horticulturalist James Priest, who have restored the splendor of this iconic garden for the world to enjoy.

I gratefully acknowledge the extensive research of Robinson scholar Sona Johnston, author of *In Monet's Light: Theodore Robinson at Giverny* and the curator of the 2004-2005 exhibition of the same name, organized by the Baltimore Museum of Art. Johnston's beautiful book – which includes detailed commentary about his paintings as well as diary excerpts, correspondence and many of his Giverny photographs – brought Robinson to life for me.

Another invaluable resource for me was a book entitled *Impressionist Giverny: A Colony of Artists, 1885-1915,* published by the Terra Foundation for American Art, in conjunction with the 2007 exhibition of the same name, in Giverny and San Diego. The history of Giverny as an art colony is exquisitely presented in this exhibition catalog, which contains the work of many of its artists-in-residence along with vintage photographs and historical documents.

It wasn't my intention to solve the mystery of Marie when I began work on this book. I'm intrigued by the way she dissolved into the mist of time, and I want her to enjoy her solace there. That said, I love the thrill of the chase when I'm researching a story. You can imagine my surprise and delight when I was in the Terra Foundation's vault, examining Robinson's original photographs, and one faded image of a woman standing by a tree caught my eye. I asked Terra's registrar Cathy Ricciardelli for her opinion, as we both examined the image under magnification, and she concurred: The woman in the photograph was indeed the same woman who appears in Robinson's photo studies for his painting *The Layette* – Marie. (The earrings and the ring on her left hand ultimately linked the images.) Unlike Robinson's other photos of Marie, which show her in profile or with her head bent, this particular image shows her face. It's with great pleasure that I share this image with you, on the last pages of the book – the first known photo portrait that reveals the mysterious Marie. It was taken in Giverny in "Gill's garden," according to Robinson. I spent several hours one afternoon peeking over Giverny's garden walls, trying to determine which house had belonged to Boston artist Mariquita Gill. A mystery I must leave for another day in my quest to earn my badge of distinction as an art-history detective.

I owe special thanks to: The Terra Foundation for American Art for giving me permission to reprint the Robinson photographs included in this book. The kind staff at the Ruth Chandler Williamson Gallery at Scripps College in Claremont, California, for sharing with me their lovely painting of Marie, entitled *La Débâcle*, which graces the book's cover – beautifully designed by graphic artist Elizabeth MacFarland of Pasadena, California. Sarah McKee for her sharp-eyed proofreading. And Dan Hull, for his sage advice, encouragement and willingness to search for Robinson paintings with me one day on the upper floors of the vast Smithsonian American Art Museum.

If you haven't yet been to Giverny, consider adding it to your destination wish list. (It's only an hour from Paris.) When you're there – or if you've already been – I hope *The Secret of Marie* adds pleasure and insight to the experience.

Last, but by no means least: Thank you, Theodore Robinson, for the beautiful paintings that you've left as your legacy. Your spirit lives on in the village you loved so much – and in me. In my cellular memory, I think there's a corpuscle of Marie.

THE LIFE OF THEODORE ROBINSON

Theodore Pierson Robinson was born in Irasburg, Vermont, on June 3, 1852. He was the third of six children of Elijah and Ellen (Brown) Robinson. During Theodore's early childhood, his father was a Methodist minister.

In 1856, the Robinson family moved to Evansville, Wisconsin. In the 1860s, Theodore attended Evansville Seminary, where he was awarded prizes in penmanship. At that age, he enjoyed sketching family members and friends. As a boy, Theodore was often incapacitated by severe asthma. (His father suffered the same affliction, which forced him to retire from the ministry.)

In 1869, with his mother's encouragement, Robinson enrolled at the Chicago Academy of Design (which later became the Art Institute of Chicago). He returned to Evansville after Chicago's Great Fire in 1871.

In 1872, Robinson traveled by train to Denver, Colorado, to recuperate from his asthmatic condition. (During a brief visit in Chicago, he sent a report to the Evansville newspaper about the reconstruction that was happening there.) Robinson's health improved while he was in Denver.

In 1874, Robinson enrolled at the National Academy of Design in New York.

In 1875, he made his first trip to France and registered for examinations at the École des Beaux-Arts in Paris.

In 1876, Robinson entered the atelier of French painter and art instructor Carolus-Duran. Other American students included John Singer Sargent, Will H. Low, J. Carroll Beckwith and Melville Dewey. That year, Robinson began his studies at the École des Beaux-Arts.

In 1877, Robinson exhibited his first painting at the Paris Salon: *Une Jeune Fille* (1877).

He spent the summer of 1877 at Grez-sur-Loing, with Robert Louis Stevenson, Will Low and American landscape painter Lowell Birge Harrison, among others.

In the fall of 1878, Robinson traveled to northern Italy – Turin, Milan, Verona, Bologna, and Venice (where it's believed he met James Abbott McNeill Whistler).

In 1879, Robinson stayed in Paris and Grez and later that year, returned to New York City.

In 1880, he spent time with his family in Evansville, Wisconsin. His mother was in failing health and died the following year.

In 1881, Robinson taught at Mrs. Sylvanus Reed's Boarding and Day School for Young Ladies in New York City. That year, he was elected to the Society of American Artists and was employed by muralist John La Farge. Robinson also began working for interior designer Prentice Treadwell of Boston. During that summer, Robinson traveled through New York State and also to Vermont with his father.

In 1882-83, Robinson continued working for Treadwell on projects in Boston; Albany, New York; Newport, Rhode

Island; and in New York City (on decorative details for the Metropolitan Opera House at 39th and Broadway). He spent the summer of 1882 painting on Nantucket Island.

In 1884, Robinson returned to France and visited the village of Barbizon, near the Fontainebleau Forest. In Paris that year, he met Marie, who became his favorite model. He did his first paintings of her the following year.

In 1885, landscape painter Ferdinand Deconchy introduced Robinson to Claude Monet. Robinson spent much of 1885-86 in France, mostly in Paris and Barbizon.

In 1887, Robinson visited Giverny, in June. His first extended stay in Giverny was documented in the Hôtel Baudy's Guest Register (September 18, 1887 - January 4, 1888). He spent time that winter in Paris with wealthy art patron John Armstrong "Archie" Chanler, a descendant of John Jacob Astor.

For the next several years, Robinson divided his time between Europe and the U.S., often spending winter and early spring in New York City where he kept a studio. From 1887-92, he spent his summers in Giverny. During the winter of 1890-91, he traveled to Italy (Rome, Frascati, Capri) and southern France (Antibes). He returned to Giverny in May 1891 and remained there until he sailed for New York in early December of that year.

In the spring of 1892, Robinson traveled to Boston for a joint exhibition with American artist Theodore Wendel, who also had painted in Giverny. Robinson sold his Giverny painting *Gossips* (1891) to Mrs. Nathaniel Thayer (née Pauline Revere) of Boston (a political activist and a direct descendant of Paul Revere).

That same year, the Society of American Artists awarded Robinson the Shaw Fund Prize for his painting *In the Sun* (1891) of a peasant woman reclining in a field. The previous year, Robinson won the Society's Webb Prize for his Giverny painting *Winter Landscape* (1889).

In May 1892, a few days before his return trip to France, Robinson received a visit from American artist J. Alden Weir, a close friend, who was concerned about rumors that Robinson planned to marry when he returned to France.

Robinson spent the summer and fall of 1892 in Giverny and produced many of his seminal works: *The Wedding March, House with Scaffolding* (depicting the residence of the Baudy family), his two paintings entitled *Willows and Wildflowers*, the *"vue de Vernon"* series (views of the town of Vernon, near Giverny), as well as paintings of the moulin: *Road by the Mill, The Old Mill (Vieux Moulin)* and *Moonlight, Giverny*. Also from that season were his last paintings of Marie: *La Débâcle, The Layette* and a variation of an earlier painting of her that was entitled *La Vachère*.

In 1892, Robinson read the novel *La Débâcle* by Émile Zola, published that year, a tragic tale about the Franco-Prussian war. Supposedly, that's the book (with the yellow cover) that Marie holds on her lap in Robinson's painting of her at the bridge by the moulin. Robinson wrote in his diary that Monet had found this painting of Marie "amusing." (It seems Monet had lost his enthusiasm for figure painting.) Robinson's *La Débâcle* was later praised by Chicago collector Potter Palmer as "brilliant."

On November 27, 1892, Robinson had lunch with Marie in Paris before sailing for New York five days later. They never saw each other again.

For the next few years until his death in 1896, Robinson's home base was his Manhattan studio, at 11 East 14th Street. Despite his frail health, Robinson traveled extensively, enjoying a wide circle of friends and acquaintances.

In March 1893, he went to Chicago to tour the site of the World's Columbian Exposition, where several of his paintings would be displayed. That year, he also traveled to Greenwich, Connecticut and Morristown, New Jersey, with American artist (and fellow Giverny painter) Henry Fitch Taylor. In Greenwich, he visited American Impressionist John Henry Twachtman, a friend who had studied painting in Paris. Robinson accompanied friend-benefactor "Archie" Chanler to his estate in Cobham, Virginia. That summer and fall, Robinson painted at Napanoch, New York, near the Delaware & Hudson Canal.

In August 1893, Robinson wrote to Monet, telling him he hoped to return to France the next year and was feeling optimistic about his future: "I am happy to be after all a little bit more successful, I mean regarding monetary affairs. I am selling enough to live modestly, and I think that it will continue. It is true that I do not have very large expenses. It is agreeable nevertheless to be a bit sure of the future, especially at my age. And I am very grateful to you dear M. Monet, your advice and words have helped me much, and at a time when I had great need. How I regret that I had not known you before, but after all, regrets are futile."

In 1894, Robinson painted at the artists' colony in Cos Cob, Connecticut. He taught a summer class for the Brooklyn Art School at Evelyn College in Princeton, New Jersey. That fall, he spent two months in Brielle, New Jersey, and wrote to Monet, comparing the Seine Valley to the Jersey shore: "Here, one sees charming things, in color, atmosphere, but almost always less graceful in line, and this is something indispensable." In that letter, Robinson expressed his hope to return to Giverny the following spring, but referred to the financial crisis in the U.S.

In 1895, Robinson taught a class at the Pennsylvania Academy of Fine Arts in Philadelphia. In February of that year, the Macbeth Gallery in New York organized Robinson's first solo exhibition. Robinson spent that summer and autumn painting and teaching in Vermont.

On February 6, 1896, Robinson wrote to Monet of his plan to return to Vermont to paint in the spring and told him about the process of making maple syrup: "All of it is done in the forest – the snow falling and you can imagine for yourself the quite picturesque scenes, the people of the region, the sleighs, the oxen, etc. a blue sky." Robinson referred again to the continuing financial crisis in the States and ended that letter with: "I really hope to see you one of these days, but when? First it is *necessary* that I do something here. So until that day, I will tell you good-by and I ask you to give my best regards to your family."

Robinson died, less than two months later, on April 2, 1896, of an acute asthma attack, at the Manhattan residence of his cousin Agnes Cheney. He was buried in Evansville, Wisconsin, where his gravestone reads: "Theodore Robinson

Impressionistic Painter 1852-1896." He was much beloved in Evansville. The local newspaper editor, who had employed young "Thad" as a typesetter, wrote of him in 1870 as he embarked on his career as an artist: "There is not a young man of cleaner habits, purer morals, or one whom Evansville would delight to honor in any calling more than Theodore Robinson." According to Evansville historian Ruth Ann Montgomery, for several years after Robinson's death, local school children visited Maple Hill Cemetery on the anniversary of his birthday, June 3, to place flowers on his grave.

The sale of Robinson's estate, in 1898, drew the interest of the wealthy Cone sisters of Baltimore. The sisters, Etta and Claribel, had been given $300 (a sizeable sum in those days) by their textile-magnate brother Moses to buy artwork for the parlor at the family home (to cheer up their mother after their father died). At the sale, an agent representing the Cone sisters purchased five Robinsons paintings, which became the cornerstone of the world-famous Cone Collection at the Baltimore Museum of Art.

Sources:

In Monet's Light: Theodore Robinson at Giverny, by Sona Johnston, © 2004 The Baltimore Museum of Art, published by Philip Wilson Publishers Ltd.

Ruth Ann Montgomery, Evansville (Wisconsin) historian

Museums and Institutions that have Works by Robinson in their Collections:

UNITED STATES

Mid-Atlantic

Metropolitan Museum of Art, New York

Brooklyn Museum

Baltimore Museum of Art

Smithsonian American Art Museum, Washington, D.C.

National Gallery of Art, Washington, D.C.

Corcoran Gallery of Art, Washington, D.C.

Hirshhorn Museum and Sculpture Garden, Washington, D.C.

Phillips Collection, Washington, D.C.

Philadelphia Museum of Art

Pennsylvania Academy of the Fine Arts, Philadelphia

Carnegie Museum of Art, Pittsburgh

Westmoreland Museum of American Art, Greensburg, Pennsylvania

Princeton University Art Museum, Princeton, New Jersey

Newark Museum, Newark, New Jersey

Montclair Art Museum, Montclair, New Jersey

Arkell Museum at Canajoharie, Canajoharie, New York

Parrish Art Museum, Watermill, New York

Fenimore Art Museum, Cooperstown, New York

Maier Museum of Art, Randolph-Macon Woman's College, Lynchburg, Virginia

New England

Museum of Art, Rhode Island School of Design,
    Providence, Rhode Island
Yale University Art Gallery, New Haven, Connecticut
Florence Griswold Museum, Old Lyme, Connecticut
Wadsworth Atheneum Museum of Art, Hartford,
    Connecticut
Mead Art Museum, Amherst College, Amherst,
    Massachusetts
Addison Gallery of American Art, Phillips Academy,
    Andover, Massachusetts
Colby College Museum of Art, Waterville, Maine

Midwest

Art Institute of Chicago
Terra Foundation of American Art, Chicago
Cincinnati Art Museum, Cincinnati, Ohio
Butler Institute of American Art, Youngstown, Ohio
Muskegon Museum of Art, Muskegon, Michigan
Detroit Institute of Arts, Detroit, Michigan
Chazen Museum of Art, Madison, Wisconsin
Roland P. Murdock Collection, Wichita Art Museum,
    Wichita, Kansas
Spencer Museum of Art, University of Kansas, Lawrence,
    Kansas
Nelson-Atkins Museum of Art, Kansas City, Missouri
Sheldon Museum of Art, Lincoln, Nebraska

South

Georgia Museum of Art, University of Georgia, Athens,
   Georgia
Columbus Museum, Columbus, Georgia
North Carolina Museum of Art, Raleigh, North Carolina

West

Los Angeles County Museum of Art, Los Angeles,
   California
Ruth Chandler Williamson Gallery, Scripps College,
   Claremont, California
Huntington Library, Art Collections, and Botanical
   Gardens, San Marino, California
Fine Arts Museum of San Francisco
San Diego Museum of Art
Seattle Art Museum

EUROPE

Museo Thyssen-Bornemisza, Madrid, Spain

Theodore Robinson,
Theodore Robinson (seated) with Kenyon Cox,
undated, Albumen print, 22.9 x 13.7 cm,
Terra Foundation for American Art,
Gift of Mr. Ira Spanierman, C1985.1.25

Claude Monet (1840-1926) in the Grande Allée of his
garden in Giverny, c. 1925

Claude Monet, with the water-lily panels,
in his Giverny studio, c. 1922. (The studio is now the
location of the Monet House and Gardens gift shop.)

Theodore Robinson, *Portrait of Monet*, c. 1888-90,
Cyanotype, 24.0 x 16.8 cm,
Terra Foundation for American Art,
Gift of Mr. Ira Spanierman, C1985.1.6

Vintage photo of an old mill (Le Moulin des Chennevières) in Giverny.

American painter Stanton Young, outside the moulin, c. early 1900s.

Theodore Robinson, *Women by the Water*, c. 1891,
Cyanotype, 19.5 x 24.1 cm,
Terra Foundation for American Art,
Gift of Mr. Ira Spanierman, C1985.1.8

Theodore Robinson, *Girl Lying in Grass*, c. 1886,
Albumen print, 10.3 x 24.1 cm,
Terra Foundation for American Art,
Gift of Mr. Ira Spanierman, C1985.1.5

Vintage postcard photo of the Hôtel Baudy, Giverny.

Vintage postcard photo of the Hôtel Baudy dining room,
painting of Marie (a study for *The Layette*) –
top row, third from left.

The Hôtel Baudy today (photos by Rebecca Bricker, 2015).

The Hôtel Baudy studio today
(photo by Rebecca Bricker, 2015).

Interior of the Hôtel Baudy painters' studio today
(photo by Rebecca Bricker, 2015).

Theodore Robinson sketching in France, undated.

Theodore Robinson, *The Layette*, c. 1892,
Cyanotype, 24.0 x 17.1 cm,
Terra Foundation for American Art,
Gift of Mr. Ira Spanierman, C1985.1.2

Theodore Robinson, *Woman Standing by a Tree*, c. 1892,
Cyanotype, 24.8 x 19.7 cm,
Terra Foundation for American Art,
Gift of Mr. Ira Spanierman, C1985.1.21

THE MYSTERIOUS MARIE

Theodore Robinson, *Woman Standing by a Tree* (detail)